Text Classics

D1036004

BOYD OXLADE was born in Sydney, and educated by the Jesuits in Ireland and at Xavier College, Melbourne. While at boarding school he developed a love of reading and began to write fiction.

Oxlade attended Monash University in Melbourne during the heady years of student protests, then lived in Carlton—for a time in a converted chicken shed—before the suburb became gentrified. He worked occasionally as a cook and as a gravedigger, but was mostly on the dole: once for nine years straight.

Hoping in vain to make some money, Oxlade wrote *Death in Brunswick*. It was published by Heinemann in 1987 and acclaimed for its finely tuned comic depiction of Melbourne's ethnically diverse northern suburbs.

He co-wrote the screenplay for a film adaptation of the novel with the director John Ruane. Released in 1991, the movie starred Sam Neill, Zoe Carides and John Clarke, and became a cult hit. Its grave-digging scene remains one of the most famous moments in Australian cinema.

Oxlade subsequently wrote screenplays and stories, 'mostly with no success'. He has had poems published in overseas magazines, and has returned to work on a project called 'Ron Elms, the Flying Butcher of Alamein'.

SHANE MALONEY is the author of the award-winning and much-loved Murray Whelan series—*Stiff, The Brush-Off, Nice Try, The Big Ask, Something Fishy* and *Sucked In*—which is characterised by a strong sense of humour, and an acute sense of Melbourne's political and cultural nuances. He has been published in the UK, Germany, France, Britain, Japan, Finland and the US.

Death in Brunswick
Boyd Oxlade

Text Publishing Melbourne Australia

textclassics.com.au
textpublishing.com.au

The Text Publishing Company
Swann House
22 William Street
Melbourne Victoria 3000
Australia

First published by William Heinemann Australia 1987
This edition published by The Text Publishing Company 2012

Cover design by WH Chong
Page design by Text
Typeset by Midland Typesetters

Printed in Australia by Griffin Press, an Accredited ISO AS/NZS 14001:2004
Environmental Management System printer

Primary print ISBN: 9781922079800
Ebook ISBN: 9781922148001
Author: Oxlade, Boyd.
Title: Death in Brunswick / by Boyd Oxlade;
introduction by Shane Maloney.
Series: Text classics.
Other Authors/Contributors: Maloney, Shane.
Dewey Number: A823.3

CONTENTS

Grave Laughter
by Shane Maloney

IN 1980, give or take, I was a booking agent in the music business, pitching rock bands to a circuit of Melbourne's inner-city pubs and outer-suburban beer barns. The bands were forever changing their names or breaking up, the money was terrible, the venues were fleapits and the promoters were vile. It was great.

The largest and most prestigious venue in the inner north was Bombay Rock, a former wedding reception centre on Sydney Road just past the Brunswick Town Hall. The Bombay's blank façade was painted black and you entered through a side street, up a flight of bare concrete stairs. The door was tended by bouncers only recently descended from the trees. Raised by pit bulls and selected for their stupidity, violence and eagerness to take offence, they took great pleasure in pitching luckless punters down the stairs headfirst like ballistic missiles. In those days, there was nothing hip about Brunswick.

Licensing regulations dictated that alcohol could only be served if accompanied by a substantial meal, so the punters got a ticket entitling them to choose either an all-leather dim-sim or a wedge of mystery pizza from a bain-marie at the bar. The food was cooked eight weeks in advance and lit like a crime scene. You had to be blind drunk or starving, or both, to go anywhere near it. But the crowd wasn't there for the cuisine and the joint was usually packed.

When I wasn't selling rock bands I occasionally took a drink at certain watering holes in the Fitz-Carlton vicinity, an area not yet entirely gentrified. Boyd Oxlade drank in some of the same places. He had a mop of black hair, the demeanour of a private schoolboy going to seed, a watchful eye and a sarcastic turn of phrase. He made for convivially misanthropic conversation over a glass or three. Apart from that, I knew nothing about him. If he had literary ambitions, he kept them under his coaster.

Eventually pub rock was killed by stand-up comedy, poker machines and food poisoning. I found other work, got older and moved into Brunswick—a suburb still industrial, ugly and woggy enough to be affordable. Boyd Oxlade drifted off my radar.

Death in Brunswick appeared in 1987, as if out of nowhere. Boyd Oxlade had been hiding his light. Set in a recognisable recent past, the novel was vivid and raffish and mordantly funny. It attracted an immediate readership. Its production for the screen seemed both natural and inevitable, and a film adaptation was released in 1991. Starring Sam Neill, Zoe Carides and John Clarke, it became the *Death in Brunswick* that most people know. The corpse-stomping scene in the graveyard remains one of the most darkly comic moments in Australian cinema, but an add-on happy ending took the sharper edge off the book.

The novel's resurrection as a Text Classic provides an opportunity for new readers to go slumming and old readers to reacquaint themselves with the flaccid Carl, one of the most unlikely protagonists in Australian literature. The title alone is worth the price of admission. Forget Venice, it declares. Step aside Mann and Mahler, Visconti and Bogarde. Here is a book primed to take the micky.

At thirty-seven, Carl is a washed-out barfly-bohemian, a man whose never-promising future is well behind him—along with a lesbian wife and their child. He can still squeeze into skinny black jeans, but his hairline is retreating and fiasco haunts his loins. At the fag end of his prospects, he slaves three days a week as the cook at a Brunswick music club called The Marquee—instantly recognisable as Bombay Rock—

and gets around, like Nora in Helen Garner's *Monkey Grip*, on an old pushbike, albeit with considerably less pleasure.

His only friend, the staunchly proletarian Dave, is a gravedigger at Coburg Cemetery with a monstrously PC shrew of a wife. Carl lusts after a sassy seventeen-year-old Greek barmaid at the club, Sophie, and owes Turkish Mustapha, his kitchen hand, money for drugs. His boss, Yanni, is a fat suck and the thuggish bouncers terrorise him. Perennially hungover and broke, Carl invites his mother to stay for a couple of weeks while she recuperates from a heart attack. She chainsmokes and plays a recording of Mahler over and over again. He resents her and steals her medication.

Carl's Brunswick is a purgatory of shoddy houses inhabited by surly, vaguely menacing immigrants. It swelters in the summer heat, empty cans rattling along its bluestone gutters. Mahler's Fifth drones in Carl's ears, and in the greasy claustrophobia of the club kitchen true romance is a handjob against the coolroom door. Carl dreams of escape to the kind of comfortable middle-class life he already despises. Only when he hits rock bottom does his luck begin to change.

> He looked at Sophie again. *My God!* He heard not so much the bat squeak of sexuality as a low cockatoo's shriek. She looked so young and healthy. *Maybe I...*

She had finished the pots and was leaning against the sink; she wore his short apron. He saw her in profile, a very Greek profile, he thought; her round, soft face was dominated by a strong hooked nose. *Jesus, what a conk!* It was a bit intimidating, really. *But what about that pouter-pigeon chest—that big shapely bum—the uniform—even the apron—God, she looks like something out of one of those magazines!*

He felt predatory—like that well-known molester of young Greek girls, Lord Byron. However, not having the social advantages of that aristocratic harasser, he put a note of special appeal into his voice:

'Sophie, listen, go and get us another drink, will you? A double, ay?'

She smiled. *God, look at those teeth.* He thought of his own: twenty-eight left and sore gums.

In the 1970s Helen Garner blazed a literary trail through an inner-urban milieu of sexual politics, drugs and drift. Boyd Oxlade's Brunswick lies a bit further down that trail, just a few years on. The low life was becoming a rite of passage and a new generation of writers stuck their heads in the bucket. By the time Andrew McGahan's *Praise* appeared in 1992 they were calling it Dirty Realism.

Brunswick is much changed since Boyd Oxlade invoked its name as an ironic counterpoint to a more famous book, a more redolent setting. The factories are gone, the houses cost a small fortune, the pizza is thin-crust artisanal and only the faintest traces remain of the feminist graffiti. But scratch beneath the hipster bars and snazzy apartment blocks and you will find, not far below the surface, that *Death in Brunswick* still haunts the place—conniving, paranoid and laughing grimly up its sleeve.

Death in Brunswick

To Sara and Sarah and Teresa

ONE

Carl was in Sydney when his mother had her first heart attack. He felt uncomfortable in that beautiful city and envied and despised the people he knew there. But after his holiday he felt guilty enough to offer to look after her for a couple of weeks.

Mrs Fitzgerald lived with her daughter and son-in-law in a large pink South Yarra town house. Carl went to his sister's one Wednesday and, rather truculent with embarrassment, repeated his offer. His sister was surprised.

'No, no, I *want* to!' he cried, disliking her pastel house and her loose expensive cotton clothes.

'Carl, you know you'll fight with her!'

'No, I won't, I swear,' he said, hopping in his eagerness to leave. 'Get her ready, I'll pick her up at four.' He paused. 'She *does* want to come, doesn't she?'

'Yes, of course she does, she's so pleased. Now don't let me down, Carl, she's not well, you know. She's only been out of hospital two weeks. And...what about your house...?'

'Jesus! Look, I'll be here at four, all right? Christ! It's only for two weeks.'

*

Carl, who usually slept late, struggled awake at seven o'clock. A high wind tossed the wattles in his untidy street and he could hear cans rolling in the gutters. It was warm and close.

He got up to find his mother making the first of innumerable cups of strong tea and smoking her first Rothman's Plain.

'Jesus, Mother, don't smoke!' He stepped down into the small dark kitchen. His mother glimmered blonde and puffy in the half-light. She slipped the cigarette into the sink and said gaily, 'Ah, sure, one won't hurt me.'

Mrs Fitzgerald thought of herself as a fey, charming Irish gentlewoman.

Carl felt a familiar mixture of disgust and pity.

'Well, have you taken your pills?'

'Yes, dear, don't fuss,' and she tottered back to bed carrying the tea. Carl noticed with irritation that she was wearing feathered mules, her hanging buttocks moving coquettishly through her nightie. *Christ! Thirteen more days.*

Carl, too tired to piss standing, sat slumped in his outdoor dunny. The door was open; grimy white brick framed grey-green inner suburban bush. Sometimes his yearning for comfort became insupportable. Sighing, he stood, pulling up his pyjama pants, thinking of picture windows, rose gardens and indoor lavatories. And so to shave: *Christ, I look tired—like an ageing blond rabbit.*

He marked his receding hairline like a man probing a decaying tooth, and with the aid of a second mirror he examined the progress of the bald patch at his crown. Was it any worse? Maybe. He put the mirror down sadly. *Now, what's today? Thursday. Shit! Work— oh no!*

A real stab of fear went through his chest. Three times a week he cooked at a rock'n'roll club. Its atmosphere of sleaze, danger and criminality, coupled with the strain and travail of cooking, carried him in the weekly rhythm of anxiety which only the true neurotic knows. *Still, another seven hours till I need to go; I won't think about it.*

He took a last look at his face, thinking of that time in middle age when you are a caricature of your own youth, and went to cheer up his mother.

By four o'clock his irritation and anxiety were intense. Thoughts of his job pressed in on him, and his mother's courage-in-adversity and false gaiety were maddening. By three he had given up trying to stop her smoking and, to make matters far worse, she had found a tape of Mahler's Fifth. Carl hated Mahler. She sat playing it in his cluttered living room.

'Such lovely music, dear.'

He looked at her with exasperation: there she sat, a fat blonde female Dirk Bogarde facing death, defeated, vain, but brave. *Jesus!*

*

At five, Carl dressed to go to work. This was an operation of some skill. The right image was important as he had lowered his age to get the job and had to dress accordingly: a black shirt buttoned to the neck, hanging over tight Levis, and ripple-soled shoes—about right. But his *hair*—now that was a more difficult problem. He combed it forward in the front and back at the sides, fluffed it at the crown with his hair drier, and applied plenty of hair gel. He looked in the mirror— satisfactorily neo-punk.

OK, onward!

'You will be all right, won't you, Mother? You know where to ring? I'll be home about eleven.'

Don't die on me, you old bag. Imagine the horror of finding her slumped, those bulging green eyes fixed in accusation, all orifices open—*Jesus!* And what would his sister say?

Mounting his rusty bike, he pedalled through Brunswick. The sky was low and grey. Past melancholy unemployed Turks he went, with their unfortunate wives muffled to the eyes in the thirty-degree heat; past decaying terrace houses daubed with feminist slogans, into Sydney Road, dodging the traffic, past the great white town hall and rows of bankrupt shops.

At last he chained his bike outside The Marquee. This establishment had previously been a Greek taverna where big-breasted blondes sang to bazouki bands and had extraordinary amounts of money pinned to their dresses; where the police were paid handsomely to ignore gambling and prostitution; where the brandy was seven dollars a glass and a good time was had by all.

But now the club was a rock'n'roll venue where the drinks were still exorbitant but the musicians were paid a pittance and nobody had a good time as far as Carl could see, and as for the rest, the funny business, well what about it? *The less I know the better.*

Unlocking the scarred back door he walked down a cluttered passage into the kitchen where he was welcomed by the foul fatty effluvia which enshroud even the cleanest commercial kitchen: that complicated perfume of mouse shit, garlic, leaking gas and the dirty bilge which sloshes round the bottom of bain-maries.

He looked around resentfully. The kitchen had once been well equipped and clean, but that was long ago; now it was squalid and nothing worked very well. There was a large coolroom, but the motor ran spasmodically; there were two big commercial stoves, but they were caked with grease and the burners half choked. The floor was a minefield of loose tiles, and the stainless-steel bench was scarred, its corners broken and dangerously sharp.

And what's on tonight?

He walked through into the empty dark club; there was a heavy smell of stale tobacco. He strained to see the menu chalked on a blackboard: 'Veg. Lasagne', 'Beef Curry', 'Ham Salad'—very Epicure. *Now stop that!* he told himself.

'A real cook always tries.' This maxim had been drummed into him by an old Scots cook at the hotel where Carl had finished his apprenticeship.

'Yes, yes, Mrs Wohlst,' the old man would say. (Mrs Wohlst was his straight man during these homilies.) 'Yes, I well remember in the last war, on the Arakan, making a *Boeuf à la mode avec Bechamel* out of condemned bully and custard powder—and they fucking loved it! Begging your pardon, Mrs Wohlst.'

Carl truly admired the old cook not only for his genuine skill but also for his ability to work with crushing hangovers. Carl's friend Dave had lent him *Down and Out in Paris and London* and Carl had recognized the kitchen philosophy, the ethos: *Se debrouiller*—'We'll get through!' You have to try.

10

The drunken old Scot had worked like this all his life and Carl, despite himself, always tried.

OK, then, Veg. Las. No. Beef Curry first—let's see what I have to work with. Unlocking the coolroom door, he crossed his fingers as he always did. No use! A kilo of fatty beef, dark and sinister, a case of pulpy tomatoes and half a packaged ham lay on a crusted shelf. Underneath was a box of limp salad greens. The rest of the coolroom was crowded with bags of heavily preserved potatoes.

God! God! What am I? Fucking Jesus Christ! 'What do you want? The miracle of the loaves and fishes?!' he screamed through the door into the empty club.

Shakily he sat down and lit a cigarette.

Why is it always like this? God! How I need a drink and more, much more, a few pills...

Carl, in his youth, had been an ecstatic consumer of every mind-altering drug he could get hold of; but now, flinching from experience like a snail, he craved only the bland delights of tequila and mogadon.

God! That reminded him, not only did he not have enough food to cook with, but he didn't have any pills to forget tonight's fiasco after it was over. How could he sleep with his mother in the house on booze alone? Mustafa—where was he?

Mustafa was Carl's kitchen hand and pill supplier— a youngish, quietish Turk. Carl didn't know much about

11

him. He had four children and a wife, and he lived in a Housing Ministry flat. Carl realized at times that Mustafa must be pretty smart. What with his job, dope money and the dole, Mustafa must be gleaning at least five hundred dollars a week from the interstices of the black economy. Most of the time, however, Carl hardly noticed him. He was always there.

But where was he?

'Anybody round?' Carl shouted through the service door.

'Yeah!'

Carl saw an enormous figure floating towards him through the gloom. A cigarette glowed nearly seven feet from the ground.

'Ah, Laurie,' Carl said nervously. 'What are youse doing in so early?'

Carl deliberately roughened his accent, Laurie being a bouncer and liable to be displeased at any sort of 'poofter' voice.

The huge lout straddled the counter with a vast creaking of black leather pants; gold sparkled on his chest and his blow-waved hair was tipped with silver.

'So early?' said Laurie, 'It's nearly quarter to six. You better get fuckin' moving, Cookie, Yanni's not too happy with you already. He reckons he's going to replace you with a pie machine.'

'Yeah, well, where's Mustafa for Christ's sake? How can I work with no kitchen man?'

'Ah, well,' said Laurie grinning. 'Sorry, pal, we had to biff the little wog last night.'

'Jesus! What the hell for?'

'He reckoned we all owe him, you included, Cookie, and he really started stacking it on an' we just gave him the big fuckin' push, you know? So. You'll just have to do without him—and hurry up! Yanni'll be in soon and he's got the fuckin' rags on.'

'Why do I work in this shithouse?' said Carl hopelessly.

'Same as why I do; lurks and perks,' said Laurie, slouching off into the darkness.

Well, fucking great! No kitchen hand, no pills, bugger all food and seventy meals to cook! Crushing his rising panic he shrugged his shoulders, muttering *'Se debrouiller'*—'I *will* get through!'

Beef Curry—right! He went to the coolroom and fetched the beef and, looking at it with distaste, laid it on a chopping board. He unwrapped his favourite knife, a Portuguese fish filleter, and trimmed most of the fat from the noisome mass. *Boy, it's really high! Still, curry...*

He cubed it, washed it with vinegar and fried it quickly, pouring away the resulting grease.

His knife flickering, he sliced half a kilo of onions and fried half slowly with as much curry powder as he dared. In went powdered beef stock, a packet of coconut and a jar of peanut butter—Malaysian

Beef Curry! He set this fraudulent stew at a low simmer.

OK! I'll add some spuds later, that'll bulk it out. Right; what's next? Vegetable lasagne—fucking no way. It was out of the question; he had no vegetables except tomatoes…but wait! Tomatoes, onions and *ham*. Ham…*Spaghetti Milanese!* There was always plenty of spag.

As always, like a soldier going into battle, Carl's panic disappeared as the action commenced. Soon the sauce was simmering on the stove with the curry and Carl was slicing salad vegetables with fair contentment.

He was shaking salad cream into a bowl of boiled potatoes, and as it landed in the bowl with an unpleasant plop the door flew open and Carl's employer waddled into the kitchen. This was Yanni, a gross youth whose pub-owning parents had bought him the club as a sort of apprenticeship to the real world of booze selling. Carl thought he looked like the picture of the young Brendan Behan on the back of *Borstal Boy*. He had the same look of cherubic dissipation, but added to this was a kind of stupid cunning. He wore a tracksuit and fur-trimmed moccasins.

'Hey, Cookie,' he cried with jovial menace. 'What's on tonight?' He stuck his fat fingers into the curry and licked them.

'Jeez, that's a bit strong!'

14

'Well, I had to cover up the taste of that rotten meat you bought. What are you trying to do, poison everyone? And shit, Yanni, there wasn't enough food there to feed the *staff*, let alone the poor bloody customers.'

'Stiff fuckin' shit, Cookie, we only serve munga here to keep the licencing boys happy—you know that.'

Carl did know it and it made his position weaker than a cook's usually is. Normally the management defers to the chef in some degree, cooks being notoriously temperamental and liable to storm out halfway through garnishing the *Julienne of Yabby with Tamarillo Sauce*.

So Carl had to whine instead of bluster: 'What about Mustafa? I got to have a kitchen man at least— who's going to be the slushy?'

'Don't worry about it, Cookie, one of the girls'll do it—and as for that Turkish sheep-fucker Mustafa! Well, you know what he was doin'? Selling drugs!' Yanni looked virtuously shocked.

'And yeah, I forgot,' said Yanni with a snigger. 'We told him you dobbed him in.' He turned heavily towards the door and by the time Carl had worked this out the fat Hellene had gone, leaving Carl to stew with the Malaysian Beef Curry.

*

By seven-thirty the temperature in the kitchen was in the high thirties and Carl could hear rumbles of thunder above the exhaust fans. The first whine of electric guitars told him that it was time to set up the servery. He went out and switched on the lights. On one side was a glass-topped salad table, on the other a bain-marie. The salad table was supposed to be refrigerated but Carl had never known it to work. Dusty plastic vine leaves half hid the rusty pipes. He filled the gaps with mushy watermelon halves, scattered some roughly sliced oranges, and added bowls of potato salad and sliced ham, garnishing the whole with aged parsley. About this moribund smorgasbord hovered the tiny insects which Carl had never seen anywhere else but around rotting fruit. He stepped back and looked at it all. *Jesus! But what can I do?*

It hurt him though.

Resentfully he switched on the bain-marie and filled the trays with curry and spaghetti sauce; this was Mustafa's job and Carl splashed his shirt doing it.

'Shit!'

He threw the pots into the sink and grabbed a dish cloth.

As he was rubbing the marks on his shirt, a short buxom young woman appeared through the gloom. She was carrying a large glass.

'Here you go, Cookie,' she said, handing him the drink. 'The boss says I'm helping you tonight.'

'Ah, Sophie—you little ripper, you! You've saved my life!'

He tasted tequila and ginger ale and poured a long column of coolness straight into his stomach. In a second he felt better and realized that he had been trembling slightly for hours.

'What do I have to do, Cookie?'

He looked at her with more attention. She wore a very short black gym slip and fishnet tights, a white shirt and a school tie.

'Jesus, Sophie, what are you got up as? You're too big a girl to get round like that, 'specially in this joint!'

'Yeah, well, Yanni, he turns round last night and he goes: "All you barmaids've got to wear your old school uniforms." It's 'cause of the Divinyls playing tomorrow night.'

'The what? The Vinyls? What's that? This is all getting a bit kinky.'

'No, Cookie, the Divinyls—you know, Chrissie Amphlett.'

'Oh, right,' Carl muttered.

He paid no attention to rock'n'roll bands these days, dividing them into the strutters and the jumpers.

He looked at Sophie again. *My God!* He heard not so much the bat squeak of sexuality as a low cockatoo's shriek. She looked so young and healthy. *Maybe I...*

'Listen, Sophie, just wash those couple of pots and I'll put the rice and pasta on—back in a minute!'

17

He hurried to the washroom and peered anxiously into the spotted mirror; his hair was holding up well, he thought.

That hair gel did the trick. Pity I can't see the back—I'll make sure I don't turn round. In the half light he didn't look more than—what? Twenty-eight? *God, maybe I could...*He felt his spirits lift higher. Tonight might be all right after all; the food wasn't too bad considering. And he *did* owe Mustafa money, so if the Turk was gone maybe that was it, and he *must* be able to score some pills *somewhere*—and then there was Sophie!

A certain lack of the self-consciousness usually found in young Greek women, coupled with heavy hints dropped by the bouncers, made her definitely available and to Carl, shy with women, availability was the scent of a bitch in season.

But I must have another drink. Now if I can get her to pinch me another, strictly against house rules, it'll mean she fancies me—or will it? He hurried back to the kitchen.

She had finished the pots and was leaning against the sink; she wore his short apron. He saw her in profile, a very Greek profile, he thought; her round, soft face was dominated by a strong hooked nose. *Jesus, what a conk!* It was a bit intimidating really. *But what about that pouter-pigeon chest—that big shapely bum—the*

18

uniform—even the apron—God, she looks like some-thing out of one of those magazines!

He felt predatory—like that well-known molester of young Greek girls, Lord Byron. However, not having the social advantages of that aristocratic harasser, he put a note of appeal into his voice:

'Sophie, listen, go and get us another drink, will you? A double, ay?'

She smiled. *God, look at those teeth.* He thought of his own: twenty-eight left and sore gums.

'Yeah, OK, Cookie,' she said good-naturedly.

'Don't get caught now,' he said as she swung out of the kitchen like the head girl at St Hilda's.

Excitedly he planned his next move. *What time is it? Seven-ten—not much time—first, pasta and rice.* He put two big pots of water on the stove, dropping a handful of salt into each. The heat near the stoves was terrific and the roar and boom of the exhaust fans made his head ache, so he retreated to the serving area. He could hear the steady electric grunt of an electric bass from overhead; a cymbal clashed—bands rehearsing. He remembered his dead father saying puzzledly:

'But they all sound the *same*.'

Carl would try to explain but his father would just say in his polite way:

'A bit quieter, please, boy, that's all.'

And Carl would turn up his record player.

19

But they do all sound the same. The guitar whine was knifing into his middle ear. *I'm sorry for torturing you with them, poor old chap—now I'm being punished.*

Sophie appeared from the gloom carrying another glass.

Sex, drugs and rock'n'roll! But what about drugs? What about Mustafa? Where *was* he going to get some stoppers?

He took the drink, and after taking a big slug:

'Everything OK? Listen, thanks a lot, Sophie.'

'No sweat, Cookie, Yanni's in his office with Laurie and the bouncers.'

'Jesus, they'll be down for their tea soon. Um, listen Sophie, can you give me a hand with something? I have to bring in a bag of rice from the passage.'

'Yeah, OK,' she said absently. 'Jeez, they're shit-house, them Abos.'

'What Abos?' said Carl, taken aback.

'That band upstairs,' said Sophie impatiently. 'It's an Abo reggae band from Northcote.'

'Oh yeah,' Carl muttered.

Vinyl, Aboriginal reggae—how long ago did I stop noticing these things?

She went through the kitchen. He followed, admiring her thick hair, gleaming blue-black under the harsh fluorescent light.

She went through the passage door and he realized with some trepidation that this was the perfect place for what? A declaration? Maybe even some foreplay! Not romantic to be sure, filled as it was with bags of rice and rusty iron compressed-air cylinders.

Quickly, before he lost his nerve, he slipped his arm around her waist and pressed himself to her sturdy body.

Quick! What can I say?

'Hey, Sophie, you're a real spunk!'

God! It sounds terrible. But she turned towards him easily; her breath was in his ear. She was laughing; he could feel the giggles shaking her.

'Jeez, Cookie, I didn't know you were like this.'

'What do you mean?'

'We all thought you was a poof.'

'Eh?' he shrieked in a high whisper. 'Well, I'm not!'

'That's all right then,' she said cheerfully, and robustly returned his embrace. He kissed her, enjoying the taste of chewing gum.

He slipped his hand up the back of her thighs and pressed her buttocks.

'I can *feel* you're not a poof.' She was laughing again. 'Come on, Cookie, better stop now, someone might come.'

'No, they won't,' Carl groaned. 'Please, Sophie.' He nuzzled her smooth neck. *What's the sexual etiquette here? Where do I go from here? More kissing? To the breasts or straight to the crotch? Oh, don't let me bugger this up!*

21

'Sophie, I really like you. I've been thinking about you since I started here.'

'Yeah?' she said doubtfully. But she made no move to break away.

'I never thought you was a poof. Really, Cookie, just you talk a bit funny, you know.'

There was a pause. In desperation he quickly moved his hand between the front of her thighs and let it rest in her crotch. He rubbed her gently through her tights. She sighed resignedly and moved her hips. His erection felt explosive, packed with potential like a torpedo. He guided her hand towards it—a little hesitation—maybe Greek girls don't...then she unbuttoned his Levis and started to wank him with purpose. His hand felt dampness. *Jesus—she* does *like me. Maybe...*

He slipped his other hand down the back of her tights and touched her warm buttocks.

'Hey, Cookie, cold hands!'

She staggered slightly and her elbow caught one of the air cylinders behind her. It rebounded against its fellows and suddenly the passage was full of noise as of iron gongs.

'Hey! That you, Cookie?' A voice came from the kitchen. 'Phone call from your Mum!'

'Oh God. Oh Jesus!'

'Off you go, Cookie,' Sophie said, smiling at him kindly in the gloom. She moved past him, hauling up her tights in a businesslike way. He followed her hopelessly, buttoning his fly. In the kitchen he found Laurie regarding him impatiently.

'Your mum's on the phone, Cookie, she sounds a bit upset.'

There was a phone near the servery and he lifted the receiver with sudden fury.

'Yes, Mother, what the hell is it? I *am* working, you know.'

'Carl, you are not to worry, dear, but I *do* feel a little strange and I wonder could you...' Her voice trailed off.

'Jesus! Mother! Look, I'll be there in a minute.'

God! My bloody sister will never forgive me. He turned to find Yanni standing by impatiently.

'What's up, Cookie? Tea ready yet?'

'Listen, Yanni, I have to go! No wait, I really do, my mum's really sick.'

'You comin' back?' Yanni said, frowning. 'Don't forget fuckin' Mustafa's not here.'

'Look, Yanni, Sophie can serve it out, it's all ready—Jesus.'

He hated to plead with the fat oaf, but waves of guilt impelled him on.

'Yeah, well, OK Cookie, if it's your mum...Off you go.'

Carl turned impatiently away and ran into the kitchen.

23

'Sophie! My mum's sick and I got to go home, can you look after things? It'll be quiet tonight, just give them plenty of rice and pasta, OK?'

'Yeah, sure, Cookie. Gee—I hope she's OK.'

He kissed her quickly—*that's one good thing anyway*—and ran outside into the warm, smelly Brunswick night.

*

He seized his bike and wheeled it swiftly into Sydney Road. There was no hope of riding it in the heavy traffic; cars were banked up at the lights, trams clattered by one after the other. It was very humid, and thunder rumbled in the distance.

He forced his way against the crowds on the footpath to a pedestrian crossing and stood waiting for the signal to change, hopping from one foot to the other.

What will I do if she...I haven't got a car—I suppose you ring the hospital. What about—what is it? Heart massage. *How do you...*

The lights changed and he ran across, the bike rattling beside him. Once off Sydney Road he was able to ride. Pumping his legs he forced the old bike up the narrow streets. They were nearly empty. Sometimes he saw a family sitting outside, talking quietly in the sticky heat. His heart raced and pounded. At last he turned into his street, wheels bouncing in the potholes, and flung the bike down outside his house. He stood for a moment gasping.

The front door was open and a shaft of light from the hall glinted on an unfamiliar car—a Mercedes. *What?*

He ran inside to meet a neat Chinese coming from his mother's bedroom. He carried an expensive leather bag and wore a beautifully cut double-breasted suit.

'Doctor Lee! How is she? Have you got an ambulance coming? Can I go in?'

The doctor with a smooth, dismissive gesture:

'Nothing to worry about, she just had a little turn—slight arhythmia. I changed her pills a little.'

His voice was Chinese-American. Carl reluctantly admired his well-dressed cool. A kind of mod inscrutability.

'You mean there's nothing wrong with her? Jesus!'

'Now, now, Mr Fitzgerald, heart attack *scared* her; better to be safe. I see her in two weeks. Make sure she doesn't smoke, you know? Goodnight.'

And he passed by and out the door. Carl heard the solid clunk of an expensive car door and the Mercedes purred off.

He stood for a while in the passage damping down his relief and anger and then, gently opening the door, he walked into her room.

It was the first time he had been in here since his mother had come and he looked around curiously. She had draped a square of silk over the bedside lamp and the light was pink and subdued. A crucifix hung on the wall beside her bed. There was a large plastic framed picture of the Virgin on her bedside table, and next to it a clutter of pill bottles. A fluffy rug covered the worn lino and a vase of everlasting daisies stood on his old chest of drawers. The door of the hulking ugly wardrobe stood open. It was lined with the flouncy girlish dresses she had always favoured.

He looked at her. Even in the dim light he could see how frightened she had been; her face was grey and loose and her grey-blonde hair lay flat. Seeing how thin it had become, he thought with digust of his own baldness. Her nightie was cut rather low, the skin between her breasts dry and crinkled.

'What's this, Mother?' he said at last. 'How do you feel?'

'Oh, I'm fine, dear, not to worry. I just got a bit of a scare. Doctor Lee was sweet to come but there is nothing really wrong. I'm just tired—be a good boy and make me a cup of tea.'

'Jesus, Mother! Oh, never mind! OK.'

He went to the kitchen and put on the kettle. *Jesus, she has been busy.*

The kitchen was unnaturally clean and tidy.

*Silly old…No wonder she's tired. She got a scare! What about me—I haven't taken that much exercise since…*His legs were shaking. *What I need is a drink.*

26

He got a bottle of tequila and took a quick drink and then another. He made the tea, feeling a little better.

He carried the cup to her room. *I suppose I should go back to work—no, I can't.*

Giving her the cup he felt, what? Virtuous, he supposed.

'I was worried, Mother.'

'I know, dear, and you're a good boy to come so quickly.'

She drank the tea and lay back puffing a little. She smiled at him. He shifted restlessly.

'You *are* a good son to me, so you are!'

He heard the fake Irish and winced.

'Ah, crap, Mum.'

'Don't call me Mum, dear, it's common. Now, what I wanted to say to you—sit down, I want to talk to you seriously.'

'No, listen, Mother, I better get back to work.'

'No, dear, just wait, this is *serious.*'

'Yeah, well, I suppose I could ring up.'

'That's right, go and ring up and bring my bag from the hall, there's a good boy.'

Jesus, thirty-seven years old and still being called a good boy. He went into the hall and found her bag. Automatically he flicked through the contents, remembering how he used to steal money from her purse when he was a kid. How she had caught him. How she had made his gentle father beat him. *How long before I heard the end of that?*

He wondered what she wanted to say now, *seriously*. God, the two weeks were going to be hell if she wanted to have serious talks all the time.

Serious. Now that was a word she hardly ever used. His mother prided herself on having a sense of humour, whatever that meant. Her favourite author was Nancy Mitford and she usually faced life with a sort of grotesquely genteel frivolity. It was the heart attack, he thought, that was serious. Still, she *was* brave, damn her.

Carl rang the club.

'Hello, Yanni?'

He could hear the clamour of rock'n'roll.

'Yeah, Carl, how's your mum, all right? It's pretty quiet so you can come in tomorrow, no worries.'

Jesus, it's human! Ah yes, but mothers are sacred, I must remember that.

'Thanks, Yanni. How's Sophie going?'

'Fine, don't worry, son.'

'Well, I'll just speak to her, OK? Just to make sure, you know.'

'Well, OK, mate, but it's real quiet. Tomorrow's the night—the Divinyls are on. I'll switch you through. Take it easy.'

Carl heard the phone switched through to the servery.

28

'Hello, Sophie, it's Carl.'

'Who?'

'You know Sophie, Carl the cook.'

Who you were pulling off an hour ago—Jesus!

'Oh, yeah,' she said. 'Hi, Cookie.'

'Is everything OK?'

'Yeah, sure, Cookie, everything's fine but I can't talk now—the bouncers want their tea.'

'Oh, OK then, Sophie. See you tomorrow night. Listen, can I ring you at home?'

'No, shit no. My dad doesn't like guys ringing up. I'll ring you, OK?'

Hooray! Carl happily gave her his number and went back to his mother's room, carrying her handbag.

*

'Now, dear, sit down. I want to speak, but first give your old mother a kiss.'

Reluctantly he bent and kissed her cheek.

'Oh dear, you do smell of the alehouse,' she said, frowning.

'Yeah, well, I had to have a drink. I'm sorry, but you gave me a shock.'

He sat on the end of the bed.

'You're not drinking too much again, are you, dear?'

'No, no, Mother. Don't worry.'

'Well, what I wanted to say to you, dear, was, tomorrow your Uncle John is coming here and I'm going to make a will.'

'Oh, Mother. Hell, you haven't got anything to leave. Anyway you're good for years yet, Doctor Lee said so.'

'No, dear, never mind about Doctor Lee, you're quite wrong. You see your grandfather left quite a lot of money. *In trust* it was. Now I *was* going to leave it to your sister, but you've been such a good boy lately, that I've decided to leave it to you.'

He stared at her.

This was all very mysterious. His grandfather, an Irish lawyer of the old type, had fathered twelve children on his silent little Bavarian Catholic wife, killing her at forty-one. Carl had seen their picture— the big dark Irishman standing with his fat hand on her narrow shoulder, her thin blonde face docile and wasted.

Although Carl knew that the old lawyer had been a man of monstrous greed and very wealthy, his mother couldn't have got more than a twelfth of whatever was riches in 1943. Besides, since his father had died broke when Carl was seventeen, his mother had lived a life of genteel, if discontented, poverty.

'Yes, dear,' she went on. 'Your grandfather didn't trust women. He was rather old-fashioned, you know.'

Yeah. Carl had heard stories of the disgusting old brute from his Uncle John, a raffish solicitor—the only one of his relations that he liked.

'I still don't understand, Mother.'

'Well, Carl, the boys got their money outright, but your aunts and I were left ours in trust for our children, to leave as we wanted. I always thought it a *little* unfair, especially as we were so poor after your dear father died. Anyway, your sister doesn't need any money with Clive doing so well with the factory, and he *has* been a little impatient with your poor old mother lately.'

Well, well, Clive's been impatient, has he? Carl smiled to himself—Clive, his sister's porcine husband, owned a fertilizer factory and had made large amounts of money from the superphosphate bounty, whatever that was. Carl hadn't spoken to him for years. Their antipathy was deep and mutual.

'Well, how much is it then? Don't tell me if you don't want to,' he muttered hurriedly.

'Well, dear, the trustees say it's much more than a hundred thousand dollars now. You see, Carl, I haven't spent any of the interest all these years and it's been mounting up.'

'Fuck! You've got to be joking.'

'Don't swear, dear,' she said automatically.

Carl stared at her as she lay back smiling shyly.

A hundred thou! His brain raced round like a slot car. *What could I do with a hundred thou! I'd be free.*

I could have my own restaurant. I could tell other poor buggers what to do. I could...

'Are you pleased, dear?'

'Yes, of course, Mother,' he said slowly. 'But you'll...I mean, you've got years yet.'

'That's up to our Heavenly Father, dear. After all, I've had a warning. That reminds me. You *will* come to church with me one Sunday, won't you, dear?'

'Yeah. Yeah. Of course, Mother. Um...Listen, I've got to...'

He had to get away and think. *God, how will I sleep tonight?* His eye strayed over the litter of pill bottles on her bedside table. *Maybe she's got something...*

'Now, Mother, if you want to go to the bathroom, I'll straighten up your bed and that.'

'Yes, I will, dear, that's a good boy.'

And she got up wearily and shuffled through the door.

Carl swiftly went through her pills—Linoxin, Digoxin, Vitamin B, Potassium. Ah! *Soneryl. That's more like it.* He took three, no four, swallowing them dryly. They were bitter and hard to get down. He wasn't quite sure what they were but he was past caring.

While he waited for them to hit, he made the bed and tidied the room in a perfunctory way.

He picked up a small, richly bound book. It was a missal stuffed with holy pictures. *She is taking this seriously now.* He was amused. His mother had always liked the idea of being a devout Catholic, but had never done much about it. *Shit! Imagine going to church with her.*

His mother returned and, wheezing, got into bed.

'Now, dear, I'll have another cup of tea and then off to sleep.'

'OK, Mother, and I'll have a drink after that news.'

'Now, Carl,' she said sternly, 'What I wanted to say to you was—the only reason I'm leaving you your grandfather's legacy is because I think you're going to be a good boy now. You know how wild you used to be with your drinking and the drugs and your poor wife and little girl—you know I had a letter from her just the other day. Reading between the lines dear, I'm sure she'd have you back…why don't you try again?'

Carl was horrified. He controlled himself with difficulty.

'Yeah, well, maybe, Mother. Listen, I have to go to bed myself soon, so I'll leave you to it. We'll have a talk in the morning.'

*

He left the room, his head spinning with pills and his mother's bombshells. Stumbling, he went out the back for a piss. Standing in the darkness he aimed vaguely in the direction of the toilet bowl.

33

Jesus, I'll have to get a light for out here. The poor old bag will break her neck. Break her neck! No, *stop it*—his thoughts slid—*a hundred thou! It must be bullshit, it must be. She's got it all wrong, I bet. She is getting old.*

One more drink. He took a pull at the tequila bottle, weaved into his bedroom and fell onto his bed fully clothed. His thoughts were slower now. They rose like bubbles of gas.

I really need that money. There was his ex-wife for instance. She wanted her maintenance payments. *Bloody lesbian bitch—Jesus, I hope she didn't mention that to Mum in her letter.* His daughter—he hadn't seen her for a year. He tried to remember her face. All he could think of was how *fair* everyone was—his mother, his wife, his daughter and himself—and how dark Sophie was. *Jesus, I think I did bugger that up. But she might ring tomorrow—the club. Bloody work! How did I end up there? Because I'm not good enough. I can't work in places like that the rest of my life—but I mightn't have to. No, it's crap—the money. It must be. Besides it could be years away. Anyway I'll ask Uncle John. Money, shit—what do I owe? Mustafa for one—what the hell's going on there? I better pay him though—who knows what contacts he's got in the dope world. But I haven't got it—this week I'll get what? A hundred and ninety—but there's the rent, the phone, and God knows what else, and I've got twenty dollars in the*

34

bank, or is it thirty. I'll have to be a reformed character now. God! If Mother ever found out about Mustafa and the pills and that—I'll have to go to church! I wonder what it's like now. Could it all be true—the will? And if it is how will I...what about Prue!

He sat up, holding his head. *I couldn't live with her again.* He lay back. *I'll go and see Dave before work tomorrow—he'll tell me what to do.*

He could hear rain falling outside as he turned over and slipped away into a deep sleep.

After what seemed five minutes, Carl woke to find his mother bending over him. She was setting a cup of tea beside his bed. He stared at her in shock. He felt like a new-born baby—his life a blank.

And then slowly, as the pills ebbed, his memory started to return. But what *was* she doing here? *Oh yeah.*

'Jesus, Mother, what time is it?'

'Time you were up, dear, it's a lovely morning.'

A beam of sunlight stabbed into his right eye.

'Jesus Christ! Mother, what time is it?'

'Nine o'clock, Carl, and don't shout at your poor old mother.'

'Oh, all right.'

'Get up soon. There's hardly a scrap of food in the house and I can't get round to the shops.'

'Yeah, OK, OK, Mother.'

He swung his legs over the side of the bed.

'Now dear, that's dirty, sleeping in your clothes. You really are…No wonder Prue couldn't bear it.'

'Mother! For Christ's…' He was about to let loose when he remembered. *The money—the will!* For some reason it seemed more *likely* this morning.

'Well, you know, Mother, I was pretty tired last night…How are you this morning?' *She looks good for another twenty years, fuck her.*

'Really quite well, dear. Now, get a move on, Carl, I'm hungry and I want my breakfast.'

She left the room and he could hear her in the kitchen making more tea. She was singing.

He sat for a while with his head in his hands.

God, those pills must have been strong—what were they? Soneryl? I went out like a…Soneryl—I must look them up—I must get old Mustafa on to them. Shit! No Mustafa.

Thirstily he drank the lukewarm tea.

What am I going to do? She's cracking the whip already—it must be true about the money otherwise she wouldn't dare. And what was that about Prue?

He stood swaying. *I must see Dave—Dave will know what to do.*

Spurred on by his mother, Carl washed, shaved, went shopping, and, while choking on two pieces of toast, watched nauseated as she ate a large breakfast— kidneys and bacon.

She lit a Rothman's Plain.

'Now, what are you going to do today, Carl?'

'Well, I have to go to work at five, but I thought I might...'

'Now, what I wanted to say to you, dear, was your Uncle John is coming at eleven and I really think you should be out.'

'But, Mother, I wanted to ask him...'

'No, dear, it's a lovely day. You should go for a walk. Besides you'd be embarrassed—now off you go, dear.'

'Oh, all right.'

He looked at her. She sat, still in her dressing gown but heavily made up, her eyes half closed against the cigarette smoke. She flicked ash into the congealing remains of her breakfast.

He looked away and got up abruptly.

'Yeah, I better go out.'

*

Gratefully he closed the front door on her. She was playing Mahler again and the triumphant music followed him up the street.

It *was* a nice day though. The humidity had gone with the rain and it was pleasantly warm. Turning into Lygon Street, he met the girls from the Red Robin sock factory coming back from their morning tea. He walked behind them for a while, watching their short

37

strong legs. He thought of Sophie. *Shit! She was going to ring.* He hesitated, then walked on.

What's the use, I'm too old for her. She was laughing at me. I'll have to find someone like Prue, I suppose—someone my age—someone tall and blonde. Anyway Mother wouldn't...

Gentle self-pity overcame him. It was not unpleasant in the warm sunlight. As he came to Stewart Street he realized that he was halfway to his friend Dave's house. *I will go and see Dave—he always makes me feel better.*

When Carl could bear to think about it, his friendship with Dave puzzled him. They were so very different. Dave was short and powerful. His arms were literally as thick as Carl's thighs. He had had polio as a child and it had left him with one leg slightly shorter than the other.

This gave him an extraordinarily solid, purposeful gait. He and Carl, with his nervous, leggy walk, looked together like a comedy duo.

Carl was totally apolitical, but Dave had been a committed revolutionary socialist all his adult life and on principle always worked at the hardest, dirtiest jobs. At the moment, to Carl's distaste, he was a gravedigger.

They did have some things in common, however: hard drinking and music. Dave loved opera with a real passion and Carl, though too fidgety to go to concerts, loved baroque chamber music. He had a good ear and some taste. They both collected early be-bop records and had a romantic devotion to Charlie 'Bird' Parker.

38

Some of the happiest nights of Carl's life had been spent with his friend, drinking huge amounts of whisky and listening to grand opera played on Dave's expensive stereo. Towards the morning they would listen to Bird and drunkenly mourn that long-dead hero.

Now these pleasant orgies had stopped. Dave had married and his wife disliked Carl. Still, Dave was Carl's only friend. Carl knew that Dave laughed at him but he really didn't mind. He had a deep respect for the other's common sense, his easy humour. Although theoretically Dave constantly suffered for the oppressed and wanted to disembowel the bourgeoisie, Carl had never met a happier, more contented man.

Soon Carl turned into Dave's street. It was poorer, grimier and more depressed than his own. There were no trees, the edges of the footpath were crumbling, half-filled potholes scarred the asphalt. Dark children played around a rusty, abandoned car, their shrill voices filling the air. *Shit! It must be school holidays. God! June might be home.*

Dave's wife was a teacher. Carl approached the house cautiously. It had been a rather pretty weatherboard cottage but Dave had three children and their depredations and Dave's indolence had led the house into irreversible decline. Broken toys littered the front path and some depressed rabbits cropped the ragged lawn. An old neutered tomcat watched them with lazy patience.

Carl couldn't see June's car so he walked up the front path, avoiding the toys and keeping an eye out for rabbit shit. He could hear opera—a swooping voice against angry discords. Dave was home.

He walked straight into the front room. Dave was sitting on an old sofa changing a baby's nappy. The baby was crying loudly; the noise was deafening.

Dave looked up and grinned. His big brown face was heavily lined and his beard and short curly hair were grey; a faded black T-shirt was stretched across his thick torso. His feet were bare and massive like a Picasso peasant's. Rude good spirits filled the room. He wiped shit off the baby's bum and deftly tucked the disposable nappy into a plastic bag. Carl averted his eyes. He saw with surprise and some envy that the music was coming from a video. A tarty-looking blonde shrieked from the screen.

'Carl, my boy, how are you, comrade?' Dave shouted above the din. 'Just in time for lunch. Have a beer! Have a baby!' And he thrust the squirming child into Carl's arms and lumbered from the room.

Carl, his mouth twisted with distaste, quickly set the baby down on the sofa.

What the hell is its name anyway? Vladimir or Germaine or is it Shulamith? No, it's a boy—Jesus, what a noise!

He found the control by the screen and turned the sound down.

40

What is it? It really isn't so bad, although it's giving me a headache. He found the cassette cover. *Lulu*. A bit modern for Dave. He pressed the off button on the video.

Lulu. It's like Lilly—I must not think about her.

Lilly was Carl's daughter. He remembered her early childhood and winced.

Dave's so good with them. I'm just not a father—Dave's so good at everything. Sometimes he shits me. Where did he get the money for that video, for instance? With three kids and everything—Jesus.

Carl was working himself up into a jealous rage when Dave came back, holding two cans of beer in one great hand and a plate of sandwiches in the other.

'Don't you like *Lulu*, my boy? Never mind, wait till you see what I got from England!'

He crammed two sandwiches into his mouth and took a big swig of beer. Carl had to smile—Dave was like a big kid. He took a sandwich and opened it cautiously.

Shit, health food bread. It always hurt his teeth. *Still.* He sat down. They ate and drank together in companionable silence for a while. *This really is a nice room.*

Books lined the walls and the sun slanted through a well-shaped bow window. The baby was quiet.

Dave finished eating and lay back, propping the baby on his gut.

41

'Where's June and the kids?' asked Carl nervously.

'Down at her mother's. Don't you worry, comrade,' said Dave, grinning. 'How are you getting on with *your* mother?'

'Ah, Dave, you wouldn't believe what it's like! I have to go to church with her on Sunday.'

'What!' Dave was convulsed with laughter.

'No, but wait, Dave. I've got to tell you. Jesus Christ!'

And Carl told his friend what had happened the previous night, leaving out only his sexual debacle. The history was punctuated by Dave's shouts of laughter. He found Carl irresistably comic. But when Carl came to the will he became quieter.

'More than a hundred thou. That's serious money. And how is she?…I mean, sorry, comrade, but how long will she last?'

'Jesus, Dave, it's not funny. You should have seen the breakfast she put away this morning. The quack reckons she's fine, and Christ, Dave, she's really cracking the whip.'

'Well, old chap,' said Dave, laughing again, 'you'll just have to cop it, won't you! Yes, a new Carl from now on, a respectable citizen. Yeah, and back with your missus it looks like.'

'Oh Dave! Don't.'

Carl was desperately trying to change the subject— Dave was no help at all.

'Anyway, Dave, talking about respectable, what about the video? I never heard of a revolutionary with a National before. And what's that? A home computer?'

'Ah well,' said Dave comfortably, 'it's for the kids.'

Carl looked at him lying back smiling. *It's all right for him!*

A new and terrible thought came to him. *Suppose the old bag wants to stay longer? Suppose I have to look after her for years—I'd go mad and that's that.*

He wrenched his mind away.

'And how's the bone yard?'

Dave worked part-time at the Coburg cemetery.

Originally he had started there as a joke, but now he thought it was one of the best jobs he had ever had.

'Great, comrade, you don't know how beautiful that place is. Lovely old trees, lots of birds, no one on your back. I'm doing a grave this arvo actually. There's an Italian funeral tomorrow. I'm going down when June comes back.'

Carl lit a cigarette nervously.

'Well, I better get back to Mum, I suppose.' *Christ, I couldn't face June today.*

'No, no, stick around, mate. I want to play you something.'

Dave got up and fed a cassette into his stereo. He sat back, his arm round the baby, and smiled happily at Carl.

There was a quick slurry of cymbals, some heavy thumping piano and then, suddenly, an alto sax burst into the room—fast, feverish and beautiful. Carl sat up in amazement.

'Jesus, that's *Bird*! But it sounds so...'

'Shush. Listen.'

The alto danced and span, mocking an awkward trumpet, and finished with a chord sequence so complex that Carl was left floundering behind. Dave stopped the machine.

'How about that!'

'It's so *clean*, it sounds like it was recorded yesterday. Where did you get it?'

'There's this guy in England—he's remastered a lot of Bird's old nightclub tapes with digital something. Anyway you can order them, and I got this one yesterday. Isn't it great? Doesn't that make you feel better?'

'Yeah, I guess so, but poor Charlie.' Carl felt sentimental and melancholy. 'Live hard, die young.'

'Jesus, Carl, don't be such a wimp!'

'No, it reminds me of work, nightclubs and that...I told you about that Mustafa. You know, the guy who gets me the pills?'

'Well, what about him?' Dave said impatiently. 'He's pissed off, hasn't he?'

'Yeah, but there's something going on there I don't know about and it worries me—that Greek prick who runs the place is as sneaky as a shithouse rat. I don't know, that place *scares* me.'

'Now, Carl, you'll be right. Just take it easy. Listen, if you have any trouble with them just ring, and I'll be down. And don't worry about your mother. Just keep on the right side of her and pretty soon she'll get sick of living over here and fuck off back to your sister—OK?'

'Jesus, Dave, would you really come down there if...'

'Yeah, but only if you really get in trouble though, Carl. Just take it easy! I don't know, you're like a chook in a thunderstorm. Now piss off, old boy, I have to go to work soon, and June'll be home in a cunt of a mood after her mum's, and you know how she likes you!'

Dave, carrying the baby, put his heavy arm about Carl's shoulder and led him out to the gate. It was getting hot.

'See you, Dave. Listen, thanks. I know I'm a bit...'

'Go on, mate,' said Dave gently. 'Just take it easy and I'll see you soon.'

Carl walked away with Charlie Parker's alto spinning in his head. *Good old Dave.*

*

Dave watched Carl's spindly figure recede into the heat haze. Shaking his head, he went inside, returning with a rug. He lay down in the sun with the baby. Soon he was dozing.

45

He was wakened by the crash of the front gate. His two little boys ran in, followed by his wife.

'Hi, Dad! Look at what Nanna gave us.'

They were both brandishing video games.

'Hey! Fantastic, kids!'

'Can we play with them now, Dad? Please?'

'Yeah, go on, boys.'

And they bolted inside. He looked lazily at his wife, who was standing over him. She was a tall stooping woman, in a T-shirt and grubby cotton pants. Her temples were shaven and her short hair was dyed orange. She had a badge over one sagging breast: 'Dead Men Don't Rape!' She peered at him shortsightedly.

'God, Dave! Look at this front yard! I *asked* you to clean it up.'

'Ah, sorry, babe. I had a bit of a snooze...'

'And look at Leon, will you! Christ, Dave!'

The baby had rabbit shit smeared over its face. She snatched it up, wiped it with the edge of her T-shirt, and began suckling it.

'And I didn't want the boys to start playing with those rotten games till we had at least had a discussion. They're so *violent,* those games. I couldn't stop Mum buying them—you know what she's like. Those boys— they're getting so—so *masculine* and you just don't help!'

She stamped her foot. The rabbits scattered.

Dave turned over onto his stomach. Watching his wife breastfeeding always turned him on and the sun was warming his groin. But this was not the time.

'Yeah, well, sorry, babe. Listen, go and put the kettle on. I have to go to work soon.'

'Oh, Dave!'

She turned and marched angrily into the house.

Dave stretched and looked at his watch. He sighed and got up. His size eleven working boots and socks were on the front verandah. Putting them on, he clumped into the house. Zaps and whistles came from the front room. He hesitated and went on. There was no time, but he just loved video games.

Going into the kitchen, he found his wife holding the baby with one hand and making the tea with the other. He held the pot for her while passing his hand over her buttocks. There was a big bulge in the front of his jeans.

'Just piss off, Dave!'

She fended him off with the baby. It started to cry.

'Now look at what you've done! And I've told you not to wear your working boots in the house. What time are you coming home, anyway?'

'About six, I s'pose,' said Dave. 'I thought I might go to the pub for a while.'

'Don't you dare. This is Friday. You *know* I've got my course on Fridays. You'll have to feed the kids.'

'Oh yeah, OK, what course is that? I forget.'

'Assertiveness Training. Jesus, Dave, you *know* that. Boys! Boys! Turn that down!'

She bustled into the front room.

Dave followed, slowly sipping his tea. He heard cries of 'Oh Mum!' as the video was stilled.

'Now go outside and play.'

The boys clattered out. He found her looking suspiciously at an ashtray.

'Who's been smoking?'

'Ah yeah. Well, Carl was round...'

'That wimpy little prick! What did he want? I'll never forgive him for what he did to poor Prue and that lovely little girl!'

'Now, babe, it wasn't all Carl's fault. I mean, Prue *is* a lesbian.'

'No wonder, and what's wrong with that, anyway?'

'Oh right, honey, yeah, but listen! How about this!'

And he told her about Carl's mother and the famous legacy.

She listened impatiently.

'Well, if he does get all that money—and I hope his mother lives for ages—I do hope Prue gets at least half. I *know* he hasn't been paying her maintenance. I'll write to her tonight. She's living in New South—on that commune, what is it? Amazon Acres.'

'Now June. You better not interfere,' Dave said, amused, but a little alarmed.

'Dave, just go to work! I've got to put the baby down and you're in the way. Go on!'

Dave trod heavily down the front path. He was limping slightly.

'Hey, Dad, where ya goin'?'

'I'm off to work, kids.'

'Can we come, Dad? We want to dig a grave!'

'Next time maybe,' he said easily.

'Don't you *dare*, Dave! You keep those kids out of that dirty place!'

June's voice, roughened by years of yelling at recalcitrant children, carried effortlessly from the house. Her pupils called her Miss Vinegar. Dave shrugged at the boys, went out the gate and climbed into his battered Holden.

*

He sat for a moment reflectively kneading his bad leg. He knew that he couldn't work as he did for too much longer—maybe he could get a job with the union. He was a good shop steward, after all. That would make June happy. He released the brake and drove off in a cloud of smoke.

Gunning the old car down into Sydney Road, he nipped neatly in front of a tram. Changing up with gusto, he drove toward Coburg enjoying the crowds out for Friday afternoon shopping: Greeks, Italians, Turks,

Lebanese, Chinese, Vietnamese. *What a place!* He was a little early so he parked the car, got out and wandered up and down Sydney Road for a while, looking at the shops and enjoying the people. He paused as he always did at a big Italian furniture store, gazing with wonder and amusement at the extravagantly carved chairs and tables. He stopped at a delicatessen and bought a quarter kilo of fetta cheese. He sat in his car eating the salty slab.

Why did Carl hate Brunswick so much? He didn't have to live round here.

He shook his head and restarted the car. Driving north up Sydney Road and turning up Bell Street, he came to the cemetery gates.

The main gate was locked. He sounded the horn and waited till the caretaker came out of his bluestone cottage and undid the padlock with a great rattling of chains.

'Hi, Bluey. How you goin'?'

The caretaker leaned in the car window. He was a bit drunk and Dave could smell heavy wafts of beer. Bluey's face was flushed and raddled, veins crawled over his pitted nose, and an incongruously youthful shock of ginger hair stood above his forehead.

'There you are, Dave. Come in to help Mick, have ya? He's got your tools.'

'Where is it, Blue? Not a sinker is it?'

'No, no, mate. She's an old one, not six foot, down in C3, in the wog section, you know.'

'All right. Ta, Blue. Listen, mate, you've started pissing on a bit early, haven't you? Don't let Bruce catch you. You know the rules. The Trust'll arsehole you if you don't watch out.'

'Ah, fuck Bruce and the Trust. You'll look after me, Dave, you're the shop steward.'

'Yeah, well. Be careful, Blue, all right? You owe me your last sub, by the way.'

'Yeah, yeah, off you go, Dave.' Bluey stepped back. 'There goes the gun gravedigger!'

The caretaker bowed mockingly and, staggering slightly, went back to his cottage. Dave drove slowly into the cemetery.

He parked the car under a huge gum and got out. The cemetery was old and nearly full. It stretched for a kilometre before him on two slight hills. To his right a wrought iron fence ran gently up and down, narrowing into the distance. The other slope was a little higher than the one on which he stood and the brow of the hill hid the end of the railings. The thickly clustered headstones seemed to run into the horizon.

He could see the flash of a spade on the other slope—that must be old Mick. He started walking down. Most of the graves were topped with weathered granite slabs sunk with time, the monuments leaning every which way, some split and broken, like discarded toys. Great old cypresses stirred softly against the blue sky. The chirp of countless sparrows and the coo of

51

pigeons nearly drowned the low hum of traffic from Bell Street. High above a hawk drifted.

Now he was walking through the oldest section: Irish Catholic. Rank grass grew over rusty iron railings and the tall Celtic crosses were spotted with lichen. As he went his eye flicked over the inscriptions: 'Patrick O'Donohue, Native of Co. Antrim. Died 1860. *Requiescat in Pace*.' 'In Loving Memory of little Tom Ryan, died aged two. 1882. And his brothers and sisters: Gervase, Sebastian, Florence (Dolly), Malachi, Brigit and Dominic...'

He walked on past a sign—'C of E and Non-conformist'. Here was a forest of stern angels, veiled urns and broken pillars. 'In Loving Memory of Michael Dawson, Saddler of Coburg, Died 1880 in his sixty-fourth year. Only Sleeping'. *You've really overslept, mate!* A great stone archangel holding a double-edged long sword brooded above the leather-worker's tomb. Dave often wondered how a Victorian artisan's family could afford these monstrosities. He supposed that there were just as many greedy undertakers round then as now.

He crunched through gravel. He was approaching the bottom of the hill. Here the graves were neater; here prosperous Edwardian burghers lay with their families. 'In Memory of James (Jim) Lang, died 1911, aged fifty-two, a much loved husband and father.' And (in fresher gold lettering) 'His wife Emily, died 1937, aged eighty-four'.

Why did women live so much longer now? They didn't in the old days. Repeated childbirth and drudgery did for them early—Dave thought of June. She'll die before me, probably of rage! We'll bury her with a loud hailer!

He sniggered and then felt remorseful, for he truly loved the termagant.

Starting to climb the hill he looked back—how pretty it was! People used to have picnics here—how odd we would think that now.

This was the start of the Italian section. It was more difficult to walk in a straight line now. It was so crowded that graves had been sunk in many of the paths. This had taken place before Dave's time; a corrupt caretaker had let the city's biggest Italian undertaker plant his defunct countrymen anywhere, like radishes. The grasping mortician had even sold grave plots twice and three times to different families, leading to much unseemly wrangling among the bereaved. After the inevitable government inquiry a Trust had taken over and ran the cemetery on sober and commercial lines. The older gravediggers remembered the former times with regret: bribery had flowed freely and the caretaker was so busy hiding his ill-gotten wealth that supervision was non-existent. The old man had stashed banknotes all over his cottage where most of it was found after his death, but Bluey spent much time tapping the walls and floors looking for hidden treasure.

Now Dave was in the midst of the Italian section, called on the caretakers' map 'Wog Cath'. Here the mortuary extravagance was Baroque, not to say Rococo. The headstones were long, low, built of expensive marble and black shiny granite. There were masses of gold lettering. Many graves had glass cabinets containing plaster statues and, disconcertingly, photographs of their occupants. On a few, by some stonemason's witchcraft, portraits of the dead were impregnated into the marble. They shimmered wraith-like in the warm sunlight. There was a profusion of plastic flowers and here and there Dave could see stout black-clad Italian women tidying, watering and praying. It made a pleasant and homely scene.

He saw old Mick now, working slowly on the hill. Dodging behind a line of shiny black slabs Dave approached him from behind.

'Get a move on, you old bugger!'

The ancient gravedigger started and flicked a spray of gravel into the air.

'Dave, Dave, you naughty boy! Good you come.'

Grinning with a line of pink gums, Mick climbed rheumatically out of the grave. He was tall and remarkably spare—his old legs were so bowed that Dave could see three tombstones between his knees.

Mick was near retirement. He had worked at the cemetery for twenty years. Dave, who had never worked anywhere more than eight or nine months, found this

54

extraordinary. The old man was a devoutly religious Hungarian Catholic and was often shocked by Dave's irreverence, and, being a 1956 expatriate, even more shocked by Dave's politics—but they got on very well. Dave was fond of him and Mick relied on Dave's muscles to do the work the old man could no longer get through. He wore a faded pair of pinstriped suit pants and a khaki shirt. Rain or shine, a waterproof hat sat on his bald head. White stubble covered his sunken cheeks.

'Easy, this one, Dave. Five foot nine only.'

He flexed his knees repeatedly like a decrepit policeman and he indicated a rusty iron probe lying nearby. This was pushed into family plots till it met the resistance of the previously buried coffin. It was marked off in feet and inches.

Dave grunted, looking at the modest grave and the low tombstone. 'Maria Di Marco D: 1954. *Ora Pro Nobis*'. A heap of marble chips and clay lay on a green plastic groundsheet draped over the next slab. The hole was about knee deep, carefully trimmed into a neat coffin shape.

'Jesus, Mick, it's a bit narrow, old mate.'

Dave stepped in, grabbing his pick and hefting it easily. He stretched and looked round.

'What a great day! No wonder you've been here, what is it? A hundred years?'

'You wait till winter comes, boy. Not so good then!'

'*Vait till Vinterre!* Go on, you old Dracula, fuck off and get some lunch. And bring back some props. This digging looks a bit soft.'

'Yes, Dave, I do that. You a good boy, but you fucking *red*.'

Mick had caught sight of the faded hammer and sickle tattooed on Dave's shoulder.

'Go on, you silly old bugger, and if you see Bluey, tell him to lay off the piss. The boss'll be around sometime this arvo to check out this hole.'

Mick shuffled off and Dave knew that he wouldn't see him for a couple of hours. The ancient Magyar had some hiding place over near the Jewish section where he went and read Hungarian newspapers in peace.

*

Dave dug out the damp clay, working easily and getting into the slow pick and shovel rhythm.

Funny how it gets wetter as you go down. There must be underground springs up here on the hill. No wonder they didn't last long, buried in this—what's clay? Acid or alkaline?

He couldn't remember. In his time at the cemetery he had not actually seen any corpses, but he had found bones, pitted and brittle. Old Mick reckoned that the coffins lasted longer than the bodies.

It was getting hotter. He took off his T-shirt; there was thick grey hair growing on his back. He was a little bored—he wished he had brought a radio. The only sounds he could hear were the birds and the soft breeze whispering around his ears. He dug on, occasionally looking up. Once, with delight, he saw a flight of rosellas flash brilliantly in and out through the trees.

An hour and a half passed. He was waist deep. The clay was getting very wet now and he had difficulty keeping the coffin shape. Where was Mick with the props? He hoped the old man hadn't gone to sleep.

He was gazing across the graves in a mindless daze when he heard a heavy tread behind him. He turned with difficulty in the narrow hole. It was Bruce, the Trust foreman, a big middle-aged man—an ex-grave-digger. He wore a plastic anorak in the hot sun and a collar and tie to show his exalted position. Dave grunted a surly greeting.

'How's it goin', Dave, gettin' there? That looks a bit sloppy. You need some props, mate.'

'Yeah. Mick's just gone to get them.'

'That's right, Dave. Ah, listen, Dave...You know you're not supposed to have your shirt off. It's Trust regs.'

The foreman looked away embarrassed.

'Oh, for fuck's sake! There's no funerals today. No one's going to swoon at the sight of *my* gorgeous body!'

'Yeah, OK, Dave. I didn't make the rules. But listen talking about regs...um...Bluey just let me in and he's definitely pissed. Now you know I don't want to arse-hole him, so have a word to him, will you. I mean, even the union won't cop that.'

'Yeah, yeah, OK,' Dave muttered. 'Anything else? I have to finish this by five.'

'Yeah, can you come in tomorrow at eleven to fill her in?'

'Yeah, sure.' *Beauty! Overtime after twelve.* Turning his back, he started work again.

The foreman coughed.

'Just one more thing.'

'Yeah, what? For Christ's sake!'

'Dave, we need a new leading hand. You know the Kiwi from St Kilda? Well, he's done his back. He'll be off for Christ knows how long. How about it? You'd have to work full-time but.'

'What! Be fucked, boss, driving round telling other poor cunts what to do and they all hate you, for what? An extra ten bucks a week? Jesus! Piss off.'

'Oh, all right! Just thought I'd ask.' Annoyed, the foreman turned away. 'You better go and wake Mick up,' he said, and trudged off.

Dave shook his head and started digging again.

Better not tell June about that! She'd have me running the whole show in a year! Leading Hand! What a con.

Soon Mick returned, pushing a barrow piled with short planks and screw props. He grunted as he dropped the handles.

'I think I see boss. What you tell him?'

'Now don't worry, Mick. I told him you just left to get the props.'

Still, Dave knew they were onto the poor old bugger. He wouldn't have put it past them to sack him to save on superannuation. He looked at the old man. He stood there, stooped, his eyes gummed with sleep.

Ah, why can't they…?

'Yeah, don't worry, Mick, just put the props in and I'll have a spell.'

The afternoon passed peacefully. By four, the grave was at Dave's eye level. He was going carefully now. He shoved the probe down. At six inches it met a slight resistance. There was a wooden thud.

'Hey, Mick, nearly there, mate, you better do the rest. I'm too heavy.'

He heaved himself out with one push of his big arms. Mick got into the hole, groaning, and scraped away at the remaining clay, throwing it out with practised flicks of his shovel, keeping his feet carefully at each side of the narrow grave shaft.

'Yeah, you too heavy for this job, Dave. You might put your foot in something you don't want!' The old man sniggered—a dank, heavy odour rose. 'You smell that? That old body water, you know?'

'Yeah, I know, Mick, get on with it.'

Soon Mick's shovel scraped the top of the coffin. He cleared it carefully. It was black and split. Mick prised at a crack. He could see wet, tattered, greyish cloth.

'Not much left of this one, I don't think. You want to see? Just be bones.'

'Get out of there, you old ghoul. I thought you had some respect for the dead.' He helped the old man out. 'You think we better take the props out, Mick?'

'No, might rain tonight. We just cover up box.'

They threw a thin layer of gravel over the coffin and packed up the tools.

They started to walk slowly back down the hill.

'You take the tools back to the shed and then you better go and hide for an hour, Mick. I'll go and have a word to Bluey.'

Mick took the barrow and bore off to the left, towards the shed built in the pretty leafy section where the Chinese were buried. There, a tiny lacquer red temple gleamed through dwarf willows. In it was a stone where devout Orientals burnt fake money for their relatives' use on the other side. Dave's workmates thought the custom barbarous and funny, but Dave, seeing the extravagance of European funerals, wasn't so sure. He often wondered what a Chinese-Australian heaven was like. *Great dim sims no doubt.* What an odd interesting place the cemetery was. *Bugger June—I'll stay here as long as I can.*

He trod back toward the front gate, plodding down and up the hills. He was a little weary. *You need a fucking motorbike in this place.* His limp was worse. He stopped for a while and massaged his knee. The weather had changed suddenly in the Melbourne way; it was becoming cloudy. The breeze had become chill; it whined around his ears, thin and bitter. Nearby a fallen-down bluestone chapel, commemorating a long-forgotten pioneer, loomed against the grey sky. Beyond was the Jewish section. *I bet that's where old Mick hangs out like a cobwebby old Transylvanian bat!* He trudged on, smiling.

He heard a radio and, coming round a great old vault, came upon two groundsmen. They were pulling up weeds in a desultory way and listening to the races. They were all that was left of the twelve gardeners that had worked here in the fifties. The decline and fall of a graveyard.

'Hi ya, Clarrie! Hi, Arthur!'

'How ya goin', Dave? Finished, have ya? Coming down the pub after?'

'No, I can't...Well yeah, all right, just for a couple.'

'Jeez, that was easy mate! OK, we'll see you down the shed at five. You seen Bluey? He's pissed out of his mind.'

'Yeah,' said Dave, frowning. 'I'm going up there now. He better not be on a bender—we've got a funeral tomorrow. See you after.' And he walked on.

Soon he was threading his way through the small area of low sandstone vaults behind the caretaker's cottage. Bluey came around the corner and stood swaying against the back wall, pissing onto a marble slab. The yellow stream flowed over 'In Loving Memory of Councillor Joseph O'Donnell. Mayor of Essendon 1933–1935. Died 1941. *RIP*'.

The caretaker was clutching a bottle of rum.

'Jesus! Bluey, get inside before someone sees you. The boss is right on to you.'

'Ah, fuck 'em all anyway, the pox-ridden cunts. Let 'em arse me. I've had this fuckin' place.'

'Well, put your dick away at least. Ah, Blue, what *are* we going to do with you? You know we've got a funeral tomorrow. You'll be ratshit. Here, come on.'

Dave took him by the arm and steered him round the corner and into the cottage.

'Here, Blue, come and lie down.'

He supported the caretaker into his bedroom. Dirty clothes and empty cans littered the floor, grey sheets were twisted on a camp bed and there was a sharp feral odour. Bluey threw off Dave's arm and glared at him, his eyes unfocused.

'Fuck you, Dave. Who are you pushing round? Here six months and he's the *gun,* the fuckin' gun grave-digger. Piss off and leave me alone.'

'Now look here, Blue, where's your spare set of keys? You're fucked, mate. I'll have to lock up tonight and open up in the morning.'

Bluey slumped onto his bed.

'Ah, I do feel crook,' he groaned. 'Yeah, all right. Good old Dave, you're a fuckin' beauty, just like somebody's mum. Where's me other keys? In the drawer in the office. Where's me Tom Thumb?'

Dave picked up the bottle.

'There you go. Hang on, give me a go.' Dave took a swig. 'Jesus! Bluey, that would kill a dog!'

'Great stuff it is, good for ya.'

Bluey drank deeply, retched and fell back, his eyes closed and his mouth open. Dave hesitated. *He'll chunder in his sleep and choke—silly old cunt. Fuck him anyway.*

*

Dave got the set of keys and walked down to the shed to sign off. The two groundsmen were there already and he could see Mick slowly approaching, past the Chinese temple.

'Here he is!' shouted Clarrie, 'The hardest worker in the graveyard game. His productivity astounds me. He digs like a *mole*!'

'An old mole,' put in Arthur.

Clarrie and Arthur were in high spirits, it being Friday.

'Where did ya hide today, Mick? In the ladies dunny? Pullin' your old dong. I tell you, Dave, he's a fuckin' old desperate!'

'You fuck off,' said Mick. 'I do plenty work, you wait till you get old.'

'Old as you! Jesus, I hope they put me down...'
Dave cut in.

'You coming to the pub, Mick?'

'No, no,' cried Clarrie. 'Last time he molested the barmaid. He's a fuckin' terror, I told you!'

'Shut up, Clarrie. You coming, Mick?'

'No, no thank you, Dave, you good boy, not like this shit.'

'Now, now, Mick. Don't take any notice of them. What's the time? Ten to five. Right! Good enough. I'm fucking off now, I don't know about you guys.'

They signed off and walked up to the cottage.

'Hang on boys, I'll just have a look at Bluey.'

Dave went in to the office. He heard loud, rattling snores. Looking into the bedroom he saw the ginger-haired sot lying flat on the floor, his mouth open. There was an overpowering stink of rum and vomit.

'Jesus,' he said, escaping into the open air. 'Bluey's right out of it. Go on, I'll lock up.'

They went through the gate and Dave fetched his car, drove it out and locked the gates.

64

'Get in, I'll drive you down the pub. Sure you won't come, Mick?'

'No, Dave, no. Bluey really drunk, huh? Silly man.'

'Can't stand a man who can't control himself,' said Arthur, virtuously. 'That Bluey'll bring us all undone.'

'You no talk,' said Mick, 'you drink all the time, lunchtime, smoko, you bad as him!'

'Ah, piss off, you silly old cunt.'

Mick, not answering, mounted his old bike and pedalled away with dignity, an ancient Gladstone bag balanced on the handlebars, his knees stuck out at right angles.

'Why don't you lay off him,' said Dave, annoyed. 'He's all right, the poor old bugger.'

'Ahh!' said Clarrie, 'He's a fuckin' old know-all. Always whingeing, fuckin' reffo. Still at least he's not a *slope*. St Kilda's all slopes now, except the leadin' hand and he's some sort of boong. Come on, let's have a beer. Me tongue's hangin' out!'

*

The pub was not too crowded. The drink-driving laws had largely stopped the after-work swill. They sat down in a quiet corner and drank the first pots in silence. Dave bought the first round.

'This'll be it for me,' he said. "I got to get home and feed the kids. The wife'll go crook if I'm late.'

'That woman's got you by the balls,' said Clarrie. 'If my missus said fuckin' boo to *me* after the pub she'd get the biggest backhander you ever saw.'

'Yeah?' Dave grunted.

Jesus, imagine hitting June! She'd belt me back and then be off to a woman's refuge like a rocket. Could I hit her? No, Jesus! I suppose I'm not really working class, not like these blokes anyway.

'What was wrong with the boss today, Dave? He's a bit shitty on you. You been *revolting* again, you fuckin' commo.' Clarrie winked at Arthur.

'Ahh! Fuck him,' said Dave. 'He wants me to go for leading hand and work full-time. I told him to stick it.'

'Jesus, Dave, I wish he'd fuckin' ask me. I been there five years and I'm still a Grade Two. What's wrong with you, Dave, is you got no *ambition*. He went to fuckin' uni, you know, Arthur.'

'Yeah, is that right? What was you doin', Dave?'

'Medicine,' said Dave shortly. 'I dropped out halfway.'

'You must have been fuckin' mad. Jesus, you'd be on what? Five hundred a week now, silly bugger.'

'Listen, Dave,' said Clarrie, 'you want to take that leading hand job, otherwise we'll probably get some wog.'

'Yeah, well, I got to go now,' said Dave, standing abruptly. 'See you Tuesday.'

'All right Dave. See you, mate.'

Dave left. He sat in his car for a while waiting for the traffic to ease. How he hated them talking like that! Their racism, their brutality, sickened him sometimes. They were like stupid dinosaurs. Was that his beloved working class? No, they weren't all like that. *Anyway, whatever I chose, I'm happy anyway.*

He started the car with an angry twist of the key and drove home.

*

The boys greeted him with enthusiasm.

'Hey, Dad! Did you bury many stiffs today?'

'One or two. You fed the rabbits yet? Come on, it's nearly teatime. Where's your mum?'

June was in the bathroom, washing the baby. He kissed her.

'You *did* go to the pub, Dave. Jesus!'

'Ah, now babe, I got home early, didn't I? What's for tea?'

'You'll have to heat it up. It's wholemeal spinach flan.'

'Jesus! Will the kids cop that?'

'They better,' she said, swirling the water vigorously round the baby. 'They've been driving me mad today with that video. Why *did* you ever buy it?'

'Junie, what would you do if I gave you a back-hander?'

'What! Now stop your silly jokes, Dave. Go and start tea. I'm late.'

Dave went into the kitchen. The flan was on a bench. It looked like a green-brown cowpat. *Still, it could be worse.* At one stage June had made them eat brown rice and seaweed till the boys rebelled. Dave used to take them on secret trips to McDonald's. He still felt a little guilty about that.

He put the loathsome object in the oven and filled a pot with potatoes. Surreptitiously he tipped in two tablespoons of salt. June caught him.

'Dave! You change that water straight away. I don't want you dying of high blood pressure and leaving me to bring up three boys on my own.'

Dave changed the water.

'Now,' she said, 'I've put a bottle in the fridge. Give Leon a feed at seven and don't let the boys stay up late.'

'Yeah, OK, Junie. See you soon.'

She bustled out.

After tea, Dave slumped into his favourite armchair and read the paper—the *Age*—*fucking capitalist press*. He was always meaning to cancel it. The baby lay on his chest sucking its bottle in a sleepy way. The boys were playing their video games again, but with the sound muted. The stereo played softly—Paul Desmond.

The baby finished its bottle.

'Hey, kids, take this to the kitchen and bring me a beer. Good boys.'

He drank from the can, occasionally giving the baby a sip. He was tired and his leg ached. Soon he fell into a light doze. The baby slept, its soft head under his chin. The boys were reading quietly: battle comics, strictly forbidden. Dave woke sometimes, savouring the peace.

At eight forty-five, his eldest son tugged at his arm.

'We're goin' to bed now, Dad. You better put Leon in his cot, otherwise Mum'll kill ya.'

'Yeah, OK, kids,' Dave mumbled. 'Good boys.'

He slept on...

'Dave! What *are* you doing?' June had returned.

'Give me that baby! Honestly, Dave, you're always either asleep or making a mess!'

She snatched the baby. It had wet his T-shirt.

'Oh well. Yeah. Sorry, babe.'

He went back to sleep.

'You coming to bed, Dave?'

'In a minute, hon.'

He slept on, the TV flickering blankly. After midnight sometime the phone rang. Dave woke with a start.

Jesus! Who's ringing at this hour? Shit. The baby'll wake up and June...

He lurched to his feet, stumbled to the phone and lifted the receiver. He could hear a strange panting noise like an animal. Then:

'Dave! Dave! You there, Dave?'

'Yeah. Who the fuck is this?'
The voice was unrecognizable.
'Dave! Come quick.'
It was Carl.

70

As Carl left Dave's street, he looked at his watch. It was only twelve. He was surprised at how early it was, then he remembered that his mother had woken him at nine. He wasn't used to getting up before eleven.

I had better go home—Uncle John mightn't have left. I might find out something more…Jesus! Thrown out of my own house!

He tried to feel indignant but he couldn't. He felt good, sort of lightheaded—a bit distant from everything—it was the music at Dave's, his friend's reassuring good humour and something else.

Maybe those pills from last night—Soneryl! I must sneak into Mother's room today and cop some more of those. Who needs Mustafa when I've got good old Mum!

Turning into Stewart Street, he saw a line of flapping posters: 'The Marquee Tonite. Friday. The Divinyls.' Each poster was plastered on top of inches of others, a palimpsest of forgotten enthusiasms. He thought of work with very little of his usual anxiety.

Bugger it. If it gets too heavy down there I'll just quit, and if they give me a hard time, I'll just call Dave. Dave could be very formidable, as Carl well knew. *Good old Dave. As he said: 'Take it easy', and I will! And Mother couldn't give me all that much trouble. After all a hundred thou is serious money—everything's all right, isn't it?*

Carl crossed his fingers. He was a great one for crossing his fingers, touching wood and similar rituals. Now he counted the lamp posts to Lygon Street. If there were more than, what?—twelve—he was all right. *One, two, three, four—shit!* There were at least fifteen.

He hurriedly turned down a lane. *Ah, it's all bullshit anyway.* But he felt the familiar cloud of impending doom.

The lane was unspeakably dirty. The refuse from take-away shops and greengrocers spilled into the gutters. There was the sweet, foul smell of decay. Nearby, acrid steam drifted from the back of a drycleaner's.

Why does Dave like it so much round here? He likes poor people. Fuck that! With some money I could get out of this shithole. He thought of leafy avenues, quiet empty streets, an occasional big car whispering by.

Suddenly a big Alsatian barked at him from an open back yard. Carl hesitated and carefully walked past, hugging the other side of the lane. He saw with relief that the dog was chained. Looking round, he threw a mouldy orange at it. It lunged in a frenzy and he hurried into Lygon Street.

Around the corner was a laundromat. A few depressed, fat women in moccasins waited by the battered machines. Up and down the street were lines of take-away shops and coffee bars, each with their group of silent card players—Greek, Turkish, Lebanese.

Outside a video game parlour was a group of husky boys, wearing sleeveless black T-shirts, on their backs in white letters 'The Young Turks'. Carl walked past them.

'Hey, mister. Got a smoke?'

'Ah, yeah, sure.'

He fumbled his cigarettes out. They all took one, grinning.

'Thanks, mate. We got a light!'

He crossed the road feeling their eyes on his back.

Shit! It's getting like New York round here—why aren't they at school? Oh yeah, holidays. I know where they'll be tonight. The Marquee. That Laurie's a prick but he sure knows how to deal with shit like that. I must stop riding home from work on my bike—I'll get thumped one night. Imagine if they got me in one of those dark streets—Jesus.

Carl, who had been bullied unmercifully at school, was deeply fearful of any sort of physical confrontation. He became paralysed and incoherent. He remembered being beaten to the ground and kicked by boys just like these. He looked back at them. Red, impotent thoughts of vengeance flickered through his mind. *Ah, forget it— the only way you could deal with pricks like that is with a fucking Magnum. I'll just have to get out—but how? At least that house is cheap.*

He turned into his street. He thought it looked worse than ever. The dusty ti-trees drooped in the hot dirty air and he saw with irritation that the rubbish hadn't been collected again. Split green plastic bags lay spilling on the kerbs.

His uncle's car wasn't there—too late. As he opened the front door, he could hear Mahler again. This time it was the Sixth. It sounded so bombastic and tasteless after the Charlie Parker tape. He could hear his mother singing along, a high tuneless keening which put his teeth on edge.

She was sitting in his lounge room wearing a tweed skirt, twin set and pearls.

Pearls! They looked real too.

He looked at them with proprietary interest. A thunderous chord came from the stereo.

'Really, Mother, do you have to play that garbage? Turn it down for God's sake.'

'Oh, there you are dear. Why? Don't you like my beautiful Mahler? You've always loved good music. I hope that club isn't spoiling your ear.'

'Yeah, well, Mother, maybe that's a good reason for leaving. I don't like that place much anyway.'

'Now Carl, I would be very unhappy if you left. Why can't you see if you can stay in a job for a reasonable time?'

'Now look here, Mother!'

'Now, dear, that isn't what I wanted to talk to you about. Your Uncle John has just left and we've finished drawing up my will. Do sit down dear, and stop fidgeting. You do want to hear, don't you?'

'Yeah, I guess so.'

'Well now,' she said, smiling at him, 'you are to get all my pennies and half my bits and pieces, but one thing. You are not to sell them. You do promise me, don't you, Carl? And that's another thing. I'd really like you to change your name back to Charles as your father and I called you. I can't think why you changed it in the first place.'

'Because, Mother, I didn't like everyone calling me Charlie. Christ! That's twenty years ago!'

'Well, dear, I think it's little enough to ask. I remember your father was very unhappy about it at

75

the time. But never mind that for now. Aren't you pleased? You'll be quite well off.'

'Yeah, of course. Yeah, I am. Listen, did you get some lunch?'

She wasn't listening.

'I feel a little tired. I think I'll lie down this afternoon. Why don't you go outside? It's a beautiful day, and your back garden needs such a lot of work.'

'Gee, Mother. I have to work tonight you know—till one o'clock.'

'Now Carl. You're a young man. You should have plenty of energy. It's just your bad habits. You had nearly a quarter of a bottle of spirits when you got home last night. I *don't* like to see you drinking so much.'

Christ! She'll be marking the bottle next. He controlled himself.

'Well, I *was* a bit upset.'

Take it easy.

'Now, dear, just try and please your old mother. I haven't got all that much time left, you know.'

'Oh Mother, Doctor Lee said you were quite well. You just have to give up those cigarettes, that's all.'

'Doctors don't know everything. Now off you go, outside—I want to have a rest.'

She turned up the music and settled back.

Carl wandered out into his back yard. It was a maze of overgrown native trees, grey-green spiny grevilleas and untidy ti-tree. Over all hung the cat's-piss smell of wattle. He found it terribly depressing. No wonder the early explorers succumbed to melancholy, surrounded by this sort of thing. He sat down on the bumpy brick paving.

He felt trapped; a Carl at bay, bailed up by circling mothers.

Maybe I could go interstate—I could say I had a job in Sydney or something. I could write to her—tell her any bullshit. No, it wouldn't work. I just haven't got the money. Anyway—he had a feeble burst of spirit—*I won't be forced out of my own house. God, listen to that awful music.*

He paced around like a prisoner in an exercise yard, whistling the alto solo from 'April in Paris'.

That's what I'd like to do—lie back and have a couple of drinks and listen to some bop. But Mother hates jazz, and as for boozing in the afternoon…! How long till work? Five hours! I'll go spare! I will—and I'll fuck things up and then I'll be sorry. Like she said, in four or five years I could be pretty well off—four or five years!

He sat down again, looking at his dilapidated outside lavatory.

What did she mean, she drew up the will? Does that mean she hasn't signed it? She'll keep it hanging over my head like a…a sword. Still, half her china and silver and that—why, that could be worth, what? Ten thou at least. You only have to look in antique shops.

77

Christ! As soon as she wheezes her last I'll have that gear in an auction so quick…! But I'll have to be a good boy till then—no wonder Dave was laughing.

Why has *she always tried to make me into something I'm not?* He remembered his kindly, ineffectual father—*she really tried it on you too, you poor old bugger.* He remembered his mother's scorn and rage when his father had gone bankrupt. *And when he took us out of those expensive schools—Jesus! We got into him too. How we must have hurt him.* Carl was filled with self pity and regret. *Well, I can't do anything about it now—ah shit, and I felt so good coming back from Dave's. Hang on, that's something I can do—nick some pills…*

He went inside. The symphony was coming to its loud and messy end. His mother was lying back with her feet up. Carl noticed with disgust the varicose veins over her shins.

'I'll just tidy up your room, Mother.'

'No need, dear,' she said, with her eyes closed. 'I did it this morning.'

'Well, you might need some flowers or something. I'll get the vase from your side table. You like boronia, don't you? There's some out the back.'

'That's very sweet of you, dear. You could put the kettle on too.'

Carl hurried into his mother's room, closing the door. He examined the bedside table. Linoxin, Kinidin—everything except Soneryl.

That's funny, where's the stoppers? Don't tell me she's a wake-up. Where...?

He saw her handbag on a chair. Quickly unfastening it, he rummaged through. *Ah ha!* He removed the plastic vial. As he did so he saw a green banded document tucked into a side pocket. *Must be the will!* Trying to unfold it with one hand, he dropped the bag and the vial. Little pink pills spilled across the floor. *Shit!* He was on his knees feverishly gathering them up when the phone rang outside the bedroom door. He heard his mother shuffle across the lounge room.

'I'll go, dear.'

Oh God.

He scooped as many pills as he could into the bottle and flicked the rest under the bed. Moving with lightning speed he tucked the will back and replaced the bag on the chair. His mother opened the door.

'For you, Carl, a young lady.'

'OK, thanks, Mother.'

He could feel sweat trickling down his back. *Jesus! That was close.* As she turned, he slipped the pills into her bag and went to the phone. It was Sophie.

'Hi, Sophie. I didn't think you'd ring.'

'Hi, Cookie. I rang this morning. Your mum answered. She said she'd tell you.'

'Oh, right, yeah...um, where are you?'

'I'm at my Auntie Martha's looking after my cousin Con. What're you doin'?'

'Nothing much. Sitting round thinking about you.'

'Oh yeah?'

'No, really. Listen, what are you doing later on?'

'I got to take Con to the movies soon. It's school holidays you know, and Auntie Martha's at work. She works at Kmart.'

'Well, I might come, OK? What are you going to?'

'*Alien BattleStar*—you don't want to see that, do you?'

'Yeah, sure. It's a kids' film, is it? I don't mind. Hey, don't you want me to come?'

'Yeah, if you want to.'

'What time then?'

'Two fifteen. You know where?'

'I'll find it. Ah…Can I meet you inside? In the foyer, I mean.'

'Yeah, OK, Cookie. I'll see you there.'

'And Sophie, please don't call me Cookie, huh?'

'OK. See you.'

He put the phone down, doing a little dance step of delight. *Hey, what about that!*

His mother came back with a cup of tea.

'Did you want one, dear?'

'No, Mother. Hey, why didn't you tell me Sophie rang?'

'It must have slipped my mind, but I don't really think you should be carrying on with other girls when you're still married to poor Prue. Your divorce isn't through yet, you know, which reminds me, I want to speak to you about that.'

'Oh Mother! That's just a girl from work. She was ringing to tell me about last night.' *Thank Christ the old bag is a bit deaf.*

'Yes, well, she sounds very common, Carl. Not like dear Prue. She sounds *foreign*. Is she Italian or something?'

'No, Mother, she's Australian. Well, Greek-Australian, and listen, I don't really want to talk about Prue. She won't let me see Lilly, you know.' *And dear Prue licks cunts—I'd love to tell you about that, you old bag.*

'What time is it? Ah, listen, Mother. I just remembered, I have to go into the city. I promised to meet someone.'

'Who, dear?' She looked at him suspiciously.

'Ah...*Dave*. Yeah, I fixed it up ages ago.'

'That *awful* Dave. Oh Carl, I thought you had given him up.'

'Jesus, Mother, come on. He's a respectable married man now. He's got three little kids and a wife and everything.'

'Yes, Carl, and I remember he used to get you into so much trouble—is he still a communist?'

'No, no, Mother. He always asks after you— um...I'll just get your flowers and then I better have a shower and get changed.'

81

Carl scurried outside, grabbed a piece of foliage from the nearest tree, and, hurrying into his mother's bedroom, shoved the spiny mass into a vase. He looked round furtively and reached under the bed, found the pills he had dropped, pocketed them, and went back into the lounge room.

'All right, Mother, I'll just have a wash and I'll be off.'

'If you *must*, Carl. I was looking forward to a quiet chat this afternoon. I've hardly seen you since I arrived.'

'Don't worry, Mother, I only have to work two hours tomorrow arvo and I'll have all Sunday free.' *Christ! What a thought—a quiet chat.*

Carl went out into his bathroom. It was a rather squalid lean-to at the back of the kitchen. Some former tenant had painted it dark green in an attempt at hiding the mould and cracks in the plaster. There was a stained bath at one end with an old-fashioned shower rose perched insecurely over it. He took off his clothes and stood in the bath, turning on the taps and waiting. The water pressure was weak and the hot water system unpredictable. Eventually there came a lukewarm trickle.

Shit! Mother must have had a bath this morning— bugger all hot water left. What a place! Still, Mother couldn't put up with this sort of thing much longer— after South Yarra! She must go back, in what? Twelve days—not that long. How everyone used to be thrilled at living in these bloody dumps—how I hate them now.

82

He remembered how he and Dave, in their youth, had shared a house in Carlton—the Latin quarter of Melbourne. Dave had been a student and Carl an apprentice. How romantic they had thought the rows of dark, crumbling terraces and the Italians and Greeks who couldn't wait to get out of them and escape to the clean air and open spaces of the outer suburbs.

The two boys had fallen easily into the raffish antinomism of middle-class inner-suburban slum life. Dave had become the socialist he still was, but Carl's revolt had never taken him beyond drugs and the cliches of the dropout. As Dave said, 'From angry youth to peevish middle age!'

Now Carl stood under the cooling water, knowing that living as he did was no longer a matter of choice. Still, he could hope.

Maybe I could cook full-time and afford some-where better—till Mother dies anyway. Then…No, I can't work full time—my nerves…I'd be drinking like a fish. At least these dumps are cheap.

He stepped out of the bath; the concrete floor felt clammy and unpleasant. On the wall facing him was a big cloudy mirror. He saw his reflection swim forward in the sub-aqueous gloom. He looked with distaste at his skinny arms and the slight pot belly beginning under his bony chest.

Ugh! I look like a fish. A rabbit fish—Sophie'll go mad, I don't think. To work!

He blew dry his thin blonde hair, teasing it carefully at the crown, applying more than the usual amount of hair gel.

After all Sophie'll be seeing me in the daylight. Thank Christ I'm seeing her in the foyer—that was good thinking. It'll be a bit darker in there—God! I can't see a thing in here.

He opened the door; hanging on the back was his mother's shower bag. He had a look inside. There was a clutter of make-up and scent bottles. He sniffed a few and dabbed one under his arms. *A bit overpowering but sexy!*

He looked in the mirror again. A cruel shaft of light from the door showed the patches of broken veins across his nose and cheeks and the puffiness under his eyes. *Jesus! Maybe I shouldn't have hit the tequila quite so hard last night.*

Looking again in his mother's bag he found some liquid make-up. Tentatively he dabbed it onto his face. The difference was impressive. He thought he looked quite healthy—a new discovery! Now he could see why old ladies wore so much slap.

I suppose it's a bit faggoty but—'desperate remedies'.

His confidence somewhat restored, he wrapped a towel round his waist and went inside.

'Dear, you are getting thin,' said his mother, as he hurried nervously through the lounge room. 'Never mind, I'll see that you eat properly from now on. If you're looking for a clean shirt, I ironed them all this morning. They were all screwed up in your chest of drawers. You really must learn to fold them.'

'Mother! Can't I even have a bit of privacy!'

'Now, dear, I thought you'd be pleased—what are you hiding in that room anyway? "We'll have no locked boxes" as the dear nuns used to say.'

'Yeah, OK. Well, sorry, Mother, thanks. It's just that my room's a bit grotty.'

The shirts were neatly stacked on his chest of drawers. He put one on, enjoying its crispness, then a clean pair of black jeans, pink socks and his ripple soles. *OK. But not quite flash enough.* He tied a scarf loosely round his neck, bandanna style. He looked in the mirror.

Not bad—will I take my leather jacket? It's pretty hot and I don't want to be sweaty...I'll carry it. What time is it? Shit! I'll be late.

'Well, goodbye, Mother. Um...I'll be going straight to work after, so I won't see you tonight. Will you be right for tea and that?'

'I suppose so, Carl. Your sister's coming over this evening. I know she'll be sorry to miss you!'

'I *do* have to go to work, Mother.'

'Yes, dear, I know. I'll see you tomorrow.'

She held up her face to be kissed. He bent over her. *Shit, she is pretty old.*

He shuffled a bit, then hurried out.

As he left, she called after him:

'Don't forget I want you to change your name back, dear. After all, it's Charles in the will!'

*

He walked to the tram fuming again.

Shit! I've been Carl for twenty years. She's just like a vampire. She wants to take my...my soul. He did feel threatened in a very basic way. *Take it easy—she'll forget about it—she better!*

In Lygon Street he bought a paper and while waiting for the tram turned to the Amusement Section.

Alien BattleStar, Cinema Centre, Bourke Street. *Oh yeah, right—how long since I've been to the pictures?* He couldn't remember. Was it a revival of *Citizen Kane*?

The tram arrived, throwing up a cloud of grit in the hot sunshine. As he got on he felt acutely self-conscious. It was full of school children on holidays and he felt that they were all staring at him. He thought he heard muffled giggles. What was wrong? *Maybe I am a bit...overdressed?* He unknotted the scarf behind the newspaper and slipped it into his pocket.

The tram ground its way a kilometre down Lygon Street into Carlton. He looked up from his paper. He thought nostalgically of his time here with Dave.

We did have a good time, but who can afford to live round here now? Doctors and bloody lawyers, that's who.

The Victorian terraces gleamed with fresh paint and brass door knobs glittered on stripped doors; in the shopping centre were lines of smart restaurants and gourmet delicatessens. *Maybe I could get a job up here.*

He dismissed the idea. He knew he just wasn't good enough any more. He looked with envy and irritation at the well-dressed groups outside fashionable coffee shops; tall leggy blondes strode into hairdressers.

The tram stopped outside the university. A single passenger got on—a tall, shabby man in middle age with long greying dark hair. He carried a shoulder bag stuffed with dog-eared books and papers. A big earring dangled from one ear.

Jesus! That looks like Paddy Smith. Carl hid behind his newspaper too late.

'Hi, Carl. Long time no see.'

'Hi, Paddy. What're you doing?'

'This and that, mate. You still cooking? Good money in that?'

'Yeah…I'm, I'm working in this flash restaurant ah…in the city. Five and a half hundred a week.'

'Yeah? Amazing! No shit! Listen mate, can you lend us ten bucks? I'm on the dole and me cheque didn't come.'

'Jesus, Paddy. I haven't got much cash on me.'

87

'All credit cards now, eh? Well how about five.'

Carl handed over the money reluctantly.

'Where you living now, Carl? We never see you round the traps any more.'

'Ah. Right. Well, I bought a house in...*Kew*. I don't get in much.'

'Well, good to see you, mate. Glad you've kicked on.'

The ageing hippie got off and the tram rumbled into the city.

Why do I do it? If I hadn't told such lies I'd be five dollars richer. Now I'll have to go to the bank. Why try and impress an arsehole like that? Jesus—look at the time! He jumped off the tram and jogged up Bourke Street looking for the cinema.

*

He arrived outside with five minutes to spare. There was a huge crowd of kids pushing and shoving. He stood panting, looking at them in dismay. Staring round wildly, he saw a pub on the other side of the road. He darted through the traffic and into the cool bar.

'A vodka and tonic thanks!'

He pulled out his money.

Shit, how much is the movies anyway? I might have to pay for her and the kid as well. He swallowed the drink thirstily.

'Give us another.'

Feeling better, he dodged back across the road and pushed his way through the mob into the foyer. There seemed to be hundreds of short dark girls with little children. His eye roved over a long queue at the ticket counter. Suddenly he saw her. She sat quietly near a video game. A little dark boy was leaping at the machine.

Carl slipped back into the crowd and found the toilets. Gazing into the mirror he felt a little dizzy— everything was slightly blurred. But he looked all right—quite healthy really. *Must be the exercise.* He went out.

'Hello, Sophie, that your cousin?'

'Hi, Carl. Yeah, that's Con. He's a real little suck. He's been driving me mad all day.'

She seemed rounder and younger than he remembered; she wore a striped T-shirt and stretch jeans.

God, look at those boobs! I'm too old—I'll be arrested!

Embarrassed he said: 'I'll just get the tickets, shall I.'

'We got ours already.'

'Oh, right. Well…'

He joined the end of the queue which was shorter now.

*Christ. Six dollars fifty! Just as well she…*He got the ticket and wandered back. Con had finished the game and joined his cousin. Carl and he looked at each other with mutual dislike.

'Hey, Soph. What's he got on his face?
Shit, you little cunt!
'Ah,' said Carl, 'I got this rash.'

'Shut up, you little suck,' said Sophie, seizing the child's hand. 'Don't you take any notice of him. Come on!' And they went into the theatre.

It was a maelstrom of noise. The film had started and every child was shrieking at the top of its voice. The screen was awash with meaningless images and the soundtrack was a huge, frightening roar.

Totally disorientated, he stumbled down the aisle after Sophie and Con. The only vacant seats were right in the front. He retained enough sense to surreptitiously kick Con out of the way and sank down next to the girl. Con's cry of rage was lost in the general clamour. He stared at the screen in total bewilderment. More for comfort than with any erotic intent he put his arm round Sophie's plump shoulders. She leaned her head to his. He smelt chewing gum. His head spinning with noise and vodka, he closed his eyes.

Despite the tumult he dozed a little. Suddenly, he was awake. He opened his eyes. Beings, creatures from his worst alcoholic nightmare, groped and slithered across the screen. His heart thumping, he hid his face in Sophie's neck.

Shit! This is a kids' show? He couldn't look, but now he *did* want to...

His hand strayed over her ripe bosom. She turned her head and he kissed her soft mouth. She responded with vigour. He felt her minty tongue pushing against his lips. Afraid she would taste his rotten teeth he closed his mouth. He squeezed a big breast. *This is more like it.* He remembered the matinees of his boyhood, the breathless excitement of his first sexual fumbles in the back row.

He slipped his hand under her T-shirt. Just then the screen exploded with light. A localised increase in the sound level showed that his advances had not gone unnoticed by the surrounding children.

'Hey mister! Want some pepper and salt?'

'Get your hand out of there. Dirty bugger!'

'Jesus, Sophie!' he cried in her ear. 'Do we have to stay here?'

'No, I seen it three times already. Con's seen it six times. Hang on. Change places.'

There was a fierce exchange between the cousins, which he couldn't hear, but he saw money change hands in the gloom fitfully lit by enormous explosions on the screen. She grabbed his hand and led him up the aisle. He heard treble voices cutting through the roar:

'Hey mister, give her one for me!'

Acutely embarrassed, he took her arm. She was shaking with laughter.

The foyer was comparatively quiet. He shook his head.

'Jesus, is that really a kids' show? I couldn't watch *Psycho* all the way through till I was twenty-five!'

'Yeah. That's nothin'. Con's seen *Night of the Living Dead* eight times on his mate's video. You should see that!'

She explained the plot of that noisome masterpiece as they got out into the street.

The sunlight struck him like a blow. He looked away, fumbled his sunglasses from his leather jacket and put them on, first wiping his face with his scarf. *Too much of that make-up. Trust that little prick to notice.*

'What about Con?'

'He's all right, he'll come on the tram. He does it all the time. He really is a little bugger. He goes: "I'll tell on you to Uncle George for carrying on with a guy". That's my dad. So I had to give him three dollars.'

*

They walked slowly up the street. She put her arm round him and slipped her hand into the back pocket of his jeans.

'Where can we go?' he asked diffidently.

'We could go to Auntie Martha's flat. She's out till six and I have to be there when Con comes back.'

She looked at him sideways with narrow black eyes.

'Yeah. Great. Let's get a cab.'

He felt an erection growing embarrassingly in his jeans.

'Oh, hang on, Sophie. You got any dough? I forgot to go to the bank. I'll pay you back tonight. You're working, aren't you?'

'It's OK. Auntie Martha's given me twenty bucks for Con.'

They hailed a cab and sat in the back. She gave the driver directions to a street in Brunswick of which Carl had never heard.

'Is that close to the club?' he asked.

'Sure is. I wouldn't miss tonight with the Divinyls. There better be a big crowd. Yanni'll go broke soon if it doesn't pick up.'

'Is that right?' said Carl, thoughtfully. 'Listen Sophie, what's going on there? What really happened with Mustafa the other night?'

She gave him a warning look and nodded toward the driver.

'Nothing. I'll tell you later.'

They sat in silence as the cab turned up Sydney Road. She held his moist hand. He remembered with sudden panic certain episodes of shaming impotence.

Maybe I wont really try. I'll just see if I could if I wanted to.

He looked at her profile. There was a bloom of fine dark hair on her upper lip. Her full mouth was slightly drawn up over her white teeth. She sat relaxed and quite composed. Despite her youth, her big Greek nose gave her real authority. He dropped her hand hopelessly.

'How *old* are you Sophie, for God's sake?'

'Seventeen. Why? How old are you?'

'Um…nearly thirty…one. I feel a bit old, compared to you, you know?'

'What for? My girlfriend Helen, she's married to this guy, thirty, and she's only sixteen. Anyway, you don't seem like as old as him.'

'Oh, right, yeah, good.'

He took her hand again. She smiled at him and tickled his palm. Starting, he looked round. The cab had turned left past the Town Hall and they were heading into West Brunswick.

Here the houses were shoddy, jerry-built, twenties villas, all crumbling stucco and ugly little diamond paned windows. On their front porches sat shapeless black clad women. The streets were wider here and papers blew about in the gritty wind. Dark clouds loomed to the west over the freeway.

The taxi drew up outside a block of red-brick flats. She paid the driver and they crunched over orange scoria spread on ragged black plastic. Discouraged palms drooped over a line of letter boxes stuffed to overflowing with advertising leaflets.

'This is a real dump!' She ran up the concrete steps. 'Come on!'

He tried to keep up with her. A studded belt was slung around her hips. He followed her round bottom. *How* do *they get those jeans on?* After the third floor, he was panting.

'Where is it, for Christ's sake?'

'Here we are,' she called down, her voice echoing in the concrete shaft. He plodded up slowly.

She was unlocking a scarred front door. There were kick marks all over the lower part.

'I bet that's young Con.'

'Yeah, but he's not really a bad kid, just a bit of a smart-arse. Shhhh now. Come in. The neighbours are real nosey round here. They're liable to tell Auntie Martha and she'll tell Dad.'

He looked round cautiously and saw a curtain move at the next flat. He slipped inside without telling her.

She shut the door. Clumsily, he grabbed her.

'Hang on. I'll just pull the curtains.' She moved away. 'Want some coffee?'

'Yeah, OK, I guess so,' he said awkwardly.

She went out. He looked around. *Jesus!* He was in a lounge room lined with what seemed a hundred icons and photographs. Melancholy Hellenic eyes followed him as he paced about restlessly.

He sat down on a low couch covered with hard slippery green plastic. Facing him was an immense TV set. On the top, he saw with interest, was a collection of bottles. He got up and looked: Metaxas brandy, ouzo and some anonymous purple liquid. Glancing round, he had a quick swig of ouzo. Its aniseed flavour reminded him of sweets. He drank again. *Wow! That's stronger than I thought.*

He heard Sophie returning and sat down.

'You like Greek coffee?'

'Yeah. I don't know. I never had any, I don't think.'

It was thick and sweet and went pleasantly with the taste of ouzo. He sat back.

'What's all these holy pictures? It's like a church!'

'Yeah,' she said, giggling. 'Auntie Martha's really holy all right. Her husband got killed back home in Cyprus and she's always trying to get hold of him. She has holy women round here all the time. They have…you know? Like in *The Exorcist*? Look, here's Uncle Nick and here's Dad.'

Carl examined the photograph.

'Which one's your dad?'

'Dad's the biggest.'

Oh yeah, he would be. A huge peasant with a heavy moustache glowered from the picture. He held a rifle in his knotty hands.

'Jeez, he looks a bit…grim. Does he give you a hard time?'

'Yeah, sometimes. I got in a bit of trouble a while ago, at school, you know, and he thinks no one's going to marry me.' She shrugged. 'Ma sticks up for me. She's

96

all right but, 'cept she doesn't speak any English and I don't speak Greek too good now.'

'What kind of trouble?'

'With this guy at school. I was going to East Brunswick High and Dad took me away and sent me to a Greek school, but I left.'

'Poor Sophie.'

He put his arm round her.

'It's OK,' she said, smiling. 'I'm pissing off from home as soon as I save enough money.'

'What does your old man think of you working at the club?'

'He knows Yanni's family. He thinks Yanni's a nice boy—the fat suck! If Dad just knew!'

'What do you mean? Jesus, that place gives me the creeps!'

Carl stood up and nervously roamed round the room.

'I'll tell you another time.' She was frowning a little. 'Don't worry about it. It's nothing to do with you.'

Carl sat down again.

'Rotten place,' he said fretfully. 'I'm leaving soon anyway.'

'Yeah? We didn't think you'd last long.'

'I'll miss *you* though, Sophie.'

'Oh yeah.'

She put her hand on the back of his neck. Taking heart, he put his arms round her and pushed his hands

97

up her T-shirt, stroking her warm smooth back, trying to work out the mechanism of her bra fastening. She arched her body against him.

I'll just go a bit further. He was haunted by memories of sexual fiasco. He gave up on the bra clip and moved to her front, cupping his hands over her breasts. *How different bras are now.* He remembered the sturdy constructions of his youth, all bones and rubber. His wife had never worn one. He thought of her aggressive pointed dugs with distaste.

Sophie leant back in his arms with her eyes closed. She sighed deeply. *Shit! I think she's enjoying it.*

'Sophie, do you really like me?'

'Yeah, of course. My girlfriend, Helen? She saw you the other day. She goes: "Carl's a real spunk, like David Bowie," with your blond hair and that. It's really nice the way it's all back at the sides.'

He passed his hand over his head, remembering to avoid his temples.

'Yeah, really. David Bowie, huh?'

Encouraged, he continued his explorations, pushing his hand down at her back.

'Ow!'

He sat up in pain; his wrist was caught in the waistband of her stretch jeans and the studded belt raked his stomach.

'Hang on,' she said smiling and stood up, unfastened the belt, unzipped her jeans and started to pull the

T-shirt over her head. His eye caught the photograph of her father.

'Hey, Sophie, shouldn't we...'

'It's all right. No one'll be here for hours.'

She dropped the T-shirt and unclipped her bra. Her breasts were very large but shapely; despite her youth they dropped a little and had light stretch marks, and they swayed a little with her movements. Her nipples were a delicious pinky-brown. Carl was overwhelmed.

Jesus—like...octopus heads! His desire faded—he sat helpless.

She sat down and unbuttoned his shirt, pushing her body against him.

'Gee, you're thin, I'm so overweight, I'll have to start going to the gym.'

'No, no,' distractedly kissing her.

She pulled him down; he felt smoothed by warm Greek flesh. *I'll have to try—she really wants to.* Sophie was breathing heavily in his ear.

He stuck his hand awkwardly into her crotch and rubbed her through her jeans. She lifted her hips and opened her legs. He pulled at her jeans ineffectually— they were so *tight*. Kicking off her sneakers, she slipped them down, raising her buttocks from the couch. He looked down—she wore dark blue cotton panties reaching to her waist. He was a little disappointed, expecting something more exotic. He attempted to draw them down but she caught his wrist.

99

'Don't look!'

She grabbed the rug hanging on the back of the couch and pulled it over them both. He felt for her groin again—she was removing her pants. His hand encountered a dense mass of springing hair. He pushed back the rug; curling black tendrils reached toward her navel, and strong stubble showed where she had shaved her thighs.

Suddenly he was unbearably excited, it was so *black*, so *thick*. She crossed her legs and looked away.

'What's wrong?'

'It's awful! I can't wear a bikini—don't look!'

'No, no, Sophie, it's beautiful, honest! Oh Jesus!'

He ran his fingers down the crisp curls and touched the soft moist outer lips.

'Oh Jesus and Mary!' he groaned, lost, and opened his fly. His erection was more than satisfactory.

He guided her hand. She encircled his cock with two fingers and caressed him gently. His fingers glided up the wetness and found a strong womanly bud; she moved her hips urgently.

All his fear was gone, he wanted desperately to fuck her and yet he could have lain like this forever with her hand on his cock. Usually, caught between impending impotence and premature ejaculation, he made his sexual encounters as short as possible, but this was so different.

He explored her wet vulva, slipping two fingers into her vagina. It felt surprisingly big—how he wanted to get in there! Carl, who was usually repelled by the normal human smells, inhaled her strong moist odour with delight.

Like…like sea shells.

'Oh Sophie!'

She smiled slightly, her eyes closed, and put his cock between her legs.

He thrust forward but there was no room for movement on the narrow couch. *Shit!*

'Wait, get up.' She slipped away. 'Gome on, get off.'

He got up, shielding his rampant penis with his hands, his jeans round his ankles.

What is *she doing?*

She leant over and pulled the bottom of the couch forward. It slid out, the back dropping, and made a bed. As she bent he saw with deep pleasure the thick black hair that sprung between her round buttocks.

'Come on then!' she said, and he sat down, a little uncertain. She pushed him back and sat astride his groin, taking his cock and sliding it expertly between her legs—it went in without hesitation.

She leaned forward and started to move her hips vigorously. She glued her mouth to his—her great breasts spread warm and soft on his narrow chest.

He felt pinned like a butterfly. He tried to move his arms. *Shit! I've still got my shirt on!*

He struggled out of it, the plastic cold on his back. Sophie slid her legs back and lay full length on him, her hips pumping.

'Oh! Oh!' she panted in his ear, 'Baby! Baby!'

Too soon the hot, delicious sensation rose from the base of his cock. *Oh no! Not yet!*

Just then a rib in the couch caught him painfully in the back. The shock steadied him and she heaved on, biting his neck with her white teeth, her pubic bone grinding into his. Looking over her olive shoulder he caught a sad icon gaze. *Jesus! Like doing it in church!*

Bemused, his hand fluttered over her bum; he felt the coarse hair on the back of her thighs—it was enough.

He came with a low cry: 'Jesus! And Mary! Oh God.'

She pumped her hips a few more times, sighed deeply and rolled off.

He turned toward her, his cock leaking a little come onto the plastic.

'Did you?...You didn't, did you?'

'No, nearly but, don't worry, it was really nice.'

She lay with her big thighs apart, her breast gently rising and falling. He could hardly get his breath:

'Oh, Sophie, I really loved it.'

She kissed him quickly and got up, wrapping the rug around her.

'You want some more coffee?'

'No thanks.'

She left the room and he heard a door close, the flushing of a toilet and running water.

What about some ouzo? He stretched luxuriously. *No, I can't be bothered getting up. That was really... wonderful!* He felt as if he had never done it before. *I've always fucked such* boyish *women.* He thought of his wife's spare figure, her sapphic tastes; he remembered the slim, small-buttocked girls of his youth. *Sophie's so ...so luscious, like one of those Italian movie stars in the fifties, like Gina...what was her name? or Anna... something...Pity she didn't...never mind, next time.*

He rubbed his cock reflectively; it stiffened some-what. Delighted at his potency he sniffed his fingers, inhaling Sophie's rich odour mixed with the chestnut tang of his come. *Jesus, I could do it again, now!*

Sophie came back carrying a glass of water.

'Got a smoke, Carl?'

'Yeah, sure, in my jacket.'

They shared a cigarette in silence.

'What time is it?' she asked.

'After four; I suppose I better go soon. What time do you start tonight, Soph?'

''Bout six thirty; I have to go home and change into my uniform.'

'You going to wear that tonight! Wow! Come down and see me, won't you? You can help me carry the rice again!'

'You're a dirty old man, like the rest of them there,' she said smiling. 'That suck Laurie was chasing me round with his thing hanging out, what there is of it.'

'Eh! That *bastard*! That's...that's *sexual harassment*.'

'Yeah, well, I used to go round with him, sort of.'

'Laurie! Ah, Jesus, Sophie!'

'Not for very long but.'

He took the glass of water from her hand and set it on the floor, pulling her down. She lay with him, her head on his shoulder. He smelt the biscuity odour of her hair.

'You don't still think I'm a...you know, what you said...a poof.'

'No, of course not, that was Laurie anyway. He goes...the other day, he goes: "That Carl's a cat", a poof you know, "and I'm gonna *snot* him one day!"'

'Jesus! *Charming*; the sooner I get out of that place the better, and you too.'

'It's not so bad, there's not many jobs round for girls, and I get plenty of tips and that.'

'I bet you do, just feel that.'

He put her hand on his hard cock. She wanked him absently, saying, 'Yeah, maybe you better leave, it *is* pretty heavy there—you know Mustafa? They really hurt him the other night.'

'Yeah, but what's...why?...oh forget it! I *am* leaving.'

He turned towards her and kissed her nipples.

'You got such *lovely* boobs.'

104

'Come on! No look, they're really *droopy*, I'm just too fat, don't look at me!'

She pulled the rug over her. He pulled it away.

'No, Sophie, you're lovely, really! Honest!'

He bent over her and kissed her round stomach and continued downward into the thick hair.

'No! Don't!'

'Why?'

'It's not hygienic.'

'What!'

'No, I don't like it.'

Carl was surprised: oral sex was an invariable ritual with all the women he had had.

'OK.'

He hugged her and put his cock between her thighs and let it rest there.

'What's your second name?' he asked.

'Papafogos, what's yours?'

'Fitzgerald.'

'What kind of name is that? You're not Australian, are you, Carl?'

'Yeah, of course,' he said, obscurely offended.

'You don't talk like a skippy but.'

'A skippy! What's that?'

'That's an *ocker*, you know?'

'Oh right, yeah, I am though.'

This settled, he stroked her back and her ample buttocks. Slipping his finger between them he tickled her anus. She pushed him away and sat up with a jerk.

'Just get away, Carl!'

'Gee, Sophie, what did I do?'

'*You* know, you're just like Greek guys, I thought you was different.'

'What do you mean?'

He looked at her in bewilderment; she was gathering her clothes.

'Sophie, please!'

'Helen's husband, Nick,' she said, looking away, 'he gets drunk and he always wants to put his thing in there, and I *won't*.'

'Ah, Soph, come on—I never...' He took her arms. 'Sophie, listen, I really, really like you.'

But he had to laugh.

'What are you laughing at, Carl, just get stuffed!'

He pulled her back on the couch.

'Ah, Sophie, calm down!'

She relaxed against him.

'Do you really like me?'

'Yeah, I sure do.'

He hugged her as tightly as he could. He slipped his hand between her legs.

'Come on, Soph, we haven't got much time.'

She sighed and held his penis again.

They lay facing each other and he pushed slowly into her. She moved with him. He gazed over her shoulder, his mind a blank as the inexorable rhythm built up. It seemed to go on for ages. She clutched his back, breathing harshly again.

'Baby! Please, baby!'

This time more urgently. He went on and on. Her vagina was looser and the pleasure not so sharp for him. She shook her head, her hair flying in his face, and kissed him clumsily. She hooked one leg round his back—he felt the heavy muscle in her thigh convulse— her cunt seemed to open and close like a great flower and he came with a slow easy pulse.

He tried to break away but she pulled him to her. Her body was wet and her breast and belly clung to him.

'You did that time, didn't you?'

'Mmm...yeah, I sure did.'

He felt a stupid pride; he wanted to shout from the windows:

'I made Sophie come!'

He lay in contentment. *I feel funny—happy!* He tried to think of something to worry about—his mother—his job—but nothing happened.

Sophie shifted uncomfortably.

'I got to go to the toilet and that, I'm not on the pill, it makes my boobs ache.'

'Oh right, OK, just wait a bit.'

He stroked her belly and thighs; they were sticky.

'No, Carl, I got to go. I had a baby before, you know.'

'No, I didn't, what?...what happened?'

'I told you, I got in trouble at school.'

'Oh right, yeah.'

'I had it and Dad made me adopt it. Now he thinks I'm a slut; he'd kill me if it happened again.'

'Christ, Sophie! This is *Australia*.'

'Yeah, but Dad doesn't know that, he thinks it's Cyprus and that. The other day he goes, he turns around and he goes, "Sophie, you get in trouble again and make your mother ashamed and I'll kill you".'

'Bloody old prick! Never mind, Soph, I'll look after you.'

'Yeah, yeah, but I still have to go.'

She left the room.

*Poor Soph. I'd like to...to...*He didn't know what. *What if she gets pregnant? Well, she could get an abortion, for Christ's sake. Anyway, she knows what to do.* He heard running water again and the toilet flush. He lay back and smoked a cigarette.

The icons gazed down on him with approval. He raised a finger to Sophie's father; the old peasant looked back with impotent rage.

Bloody Greeks! I'll leave that place tonight, bugger it, and I'll get a proper job with lots of money and I'll stop drinking so much and taking stoppers and that and...I can't wait for Mother to snuff it, I must make some money, then I could...I could take Sophie out, yeah.

108

He sighed and stretched himself; he could smell his sweat. *Shit, I need a shower.*

Sophie came back. She had a short towel wound tightly round above her breasts. She stooped and picked up her clothes, her bottom appearing distractingly. He reached for her.

'Hey, come on, Carl, it's getting late.'

Her body was damp and cool. She stroked his neck and pushed him away, repeating,

'It's getting late, you better get dressed, I got to clean up.'

'Shit, why? I don't give a fuck if I'm late, bugger them! Come here!'

'No, Carl—come on, Con'll be back soon and if he sees you he'll go, "I'll tell Uncle George," and I'll have to pay him more.'

'Little bugger! Jesus!'

He got up unwillingly, pulling his jeans up. He noticed with surprise that he still had his shoes on. *Christ! That's a bit off.*

'Um, Sophie, I hope you don't think that…'

'What?'

'Well, that I got you here just for…you know… *sex*. 'Cause I really like you and that.'

'Well, didn't you?' She was laughing. 'Anyway I got *you* here, didn't I?'

'Yeah, I guess so.'

'Go on, love. I'll see you tonight.'

'Yeah, OK.'

He put his shirt on. *Jesus! I do stink—still I'm only going to work.* He picked up his jacket. As he did so he noticed a silent sticky pool on the green plastic; while Sophie was walking to the door he wiped it up quickly with his scarf.

She waited by the door.

'OK, Soph, see you later.'

He kissed her and she tucked his shirt in at the back.

'Listen, you'll bring me down a drink tonight, won't you, Soph, please.'

'Yeah, if I can, but we're going to be real busy.'

'Well, OK, then.'

'Go on.'

She gave him a little push out the door and closed it.

He remembered the neighbours and looked around carefully before running down the stairs. As he reached the street he saw that the weather had changed, the sky was grey and a cold wind blew from the west. He put on his jacket, shivering.

*

Now, where the fuck am I? He started up the street. A gang of boys were skylarking on the corner; he hesitated and made to cross the road. *No, fuck 'em.*

He marched on and through them, turning up the collar of his leather jacket.

Reaching Dawson Street he turned right. He could see the enormous white pile of the town hall in the distance. As he walked along he noticed a tall, blonde, defeated-looking woman pushing a pram on the other side of the road. *She looks like Prue. Fuck her—she'll get no money out of me.*

But what about his daughter? He strained to remember what she looked like; he had a vague impression of white-blonde hair and pretty hazel eyes. He remembered the blue denim overalls she had worn when his wife took her for the last time.

Poor little bugger—he was flooded with easy pity. *I suppose she needs money. I must get a better job. I didn't treat her…no, it was that fucking Prue's fault—it was! If me and…and someone like Sophie had a kid, I'd be different, I'd help and everything—I'd look after it.*

A little shocked at the direction his thoughts were taking, he shook himself and hurried on in the chill wind.

Take it easy! Jesus, I only had a stray screw! Yeah, but it was so good—I was good, she really liked it—I made Sophie come!

He did a little soft-shoe on the pavement. Then he looked around self-consciously and looking up at the town hall clock stepped out soberly. *Five fifteen. Late*

111

again—stiff shit! He turned into Basilisk Street and walked toward the club feeling for his keys.

Yanni's souped-up panel van was parked by the kerb, squatting like a black toad, flickering red flames painted down the side. A line of new posters flapped in the wind: 'The Divinyls with Chrissie Amphlett.' He saw a picture of a tall blonde girl, her hair tossing wildly. She wore a gym slip and lace stockings, her garters showing on her slim legs.

Ah! Now I get Sophie's uniform. Silly buggers! What is this? A playboy club? They just better leave her alone.

He unlocked the side door and walked down the passage past the row of iron gas bottles and into the kitchen. *Shit!* It was incredibly dirty and cluttered. There was rice and pasta shells all over the floor; crushed pots crowded the stove and the sink was piled with dirty dishes.

Jesus, this is the fucking limit! He plunged through the kitchen and into the darkened club. Groping through the gloom, he ran up the stairs and passed the bar. He paused, breathing the stink of old cigarette smoke and stale booze, and glanced longingly at the bottles behind the counter, but a heavy steel grille was padlocked to the front.

Yanni's office was down a dingy passage, the door painted a streaky purple with a big sign pinned to it: 'Keep Out, This Means You.' A murmur of conversation punctuated with barking laughter came from inside.

He knocked firmly.

'Who the fuck is it?'

'Carl.'

'Piss off.'

'No—come on Yanni, I got to see you.'

'Hang on.'

After a minute the door opened. It was Laurie.

'Come in and don't make the fuckin' draught.'

Carl went in. The tiny room was crowded; Yanni sat behind his desk, his fat body crammed into a swivel chair. The whole crew of bouncers were sitting sprawled around, their long legs thrust out, blocking Carl's way. There was a sharp acrid odour in the smoky air. On the desk was a mirror, a thin line of white powder across it; a straw and a dismembered cigarette lay beside.

'What's up, Cookie?' Yanni's voice was a little slurred. He looked at Carl under his heavy eyelids.

'Look, Yanni, that fuckin' kitchen's a brothel. *I'm* not cleaning it up, you know.'

'Yeah, well you'll have to, mate, I couldn't get anyone instead of Mustafa and the girls are too busy.'

Yanni seemed a bit apologetic but Laurie cut in.

'Fuck you, Cookie, you want a job? You fuckin' well clean up, all right?'

He jabbed a stiff finger into Carl's chest. It hurt.

'Well, Jesus.'

Carl was going to walk out but he remembered his pay.

'Well, OK, just this once. What's on tonight anyway?'

'Pizza, mate, and chips.'

'What! Fuck it, I'm not a short-order cook. Fair go Yanni.'

Laurie broke in again.

'You've been fuckin' *told*, Cookie. You're just here to keep the liquor boys sweet, and anyway kids want pizza and that, what's the matter, can't you fuckin' *make* pizza?'

'Yeah, 'course I can, but what out of, though?'

'Tony went down this arvo and got all the makings, didn't you, wop?'

'Yeah,' said Tony, a handsome boy with dark curls falling to his shoulders. 'Tomato paste, mozzarella and everythink.'

'Well, gee,' said Carl weakly, 'I hope we're not too busy.'

He just wanted to get out.

'We'd fuckin' better be,' Yanni said, 'otherwise we're all rooted. Now off you go, Cookie.'

Carl turned to leave.

'And forget about this.' Yanni gestured at the white powder.

'I don't care,' said Carl, 'nothing to do with me—I'm not involved.'

'Oh yes you are,' said Laurie, 'we know about you and that arse Mustafa.'

'What! What about me and...?'

'Get going, Cookie, you're late.'

Laurie took him by the shoulder and propelled him out of the office and into the passage.

'Listen, sport,' he said, his face leaning into Carl's, 'You keep your mouth shut and do the right thing down there or I'll fuckin' give it to you—I don't like give-ups, get me?'

'Yeah, yeah.'

Carl pushed away the big man's arm and escaped.

'Hey, Cookie! We want pizza at six-thirty, so you have it ready!'

Carl looked back. The bouncer was framed in the office door; light gleamed on his leather trousers and glinted off the studs set in a wide black wristband. Laurie turned and went back into the office, his shoulders filling the door.

Carl was shaken by impotent rage and fear. He stumbled down the stairs and back into the kitchen. He crunched his way over dry pasta shells to the dry store near the toilet. Tony's purchases were in a cardboard box near the door; he turned them over—tomato paste, mozzarella. Suddenly he was struck by the repulsive memory of some cooking school folklore. 'The Cook's Revenge.' *Pizza! I'll give 'em pizza!*

He looked round the kitchen. *Jesus, where do I start?*

He fetched a broom and swept the debris into a corner, quickly washed one of the filthy pots and hid the rest in a cupboard. *The plates can wait.*

As he straightened up from the cupboard he felt dizzy. Suddenly he was shaking—Laurie had really frightened him. He sat down for a moment and thought.

Just let me get through tonight, please, and I'll never see this place again. Still, I better keep them sweet. OK!

He got up and opened the flour bin; the chalky flour was full of small black lumps. *Jesus! Looks like a mouse's sandbox.*

He was seized by a wild hilarity. Shovelling the contaminated flour into a bowl, he opened a packet of yeast and pinched some into a jug. *Now warm water. No! Not water.*

He looked carefully through the kitchen door, unzipped his jeans and pissed into the jug. I wonder if piss kills yeast? No, obviously not. The mixture started to fizz.

Adding the yeast, salt, sugar and oil he mixed, kneaded and beat back the dough. Leaving it to rise, he wandered round the kitchen thinking about pizza toppings and chips. He unlocked the coolroom door, pulled out a bag of potatoes and looked for ham. The coolroom motor was silent and there was a thick musty odour. *Dear! Dear! The coolroom's broken down; this ham'll be nice and ripe. Good!*

He sliced and chopped the ham quickly and grated some onion. The dough had risen slightly; he rolled it out. What about baking trays?

He opened the oven doors. Filthy, crusted grease traps lined the bottoms. He pulled them free with an effort, gave them a cursory scrape and laid out the dough.

I better make them good and tasty, keep the boys happy!

He spread tomato paste, scattered the ham, onion and mozzarella, and threw on some tinned mushrooms. *Shit! The silly bugger forgot olives.* He thought for a moment. *Will I? Yeah, the finishing touch!*

He smoked two cigarettes quickly till the breath caught in his lungs. Hawking up phlegm from the bottom of his chest, he spat copiously into a jug and spread the sticky liquid over the pizzas.

He stood back and looked at them. Despite himself, he felt a little shame. The admonitions of his Scots teacher, a sort of culinary superego, came to him: 'A good cook always tries.' *Well, I am trying—I'm trying to poison the buggers! Besides, these are just for them— I'll make good ones for the poor bloody customers.*

He put the pizzas into the oven and started moodily slicing chips. He hated cooking chips—it was perhaps the most dangerous job in the kitchen, and he had a livid scar on his wrist to prove it. *Fuck it, I'm not getting burnt for those pricks! I'll make oven fries, who cares if they're greasy.*

He passed the chips through a bowl of oil and strewed them onto a baking tray. Then he opened the oven door; the pizzas were bubbling and beginning to turn brown at the edges. *Jesus, they look almost good enough to eat!*

Turning down the oven slightly, he slid the chip tray onto the top rack, closed the doors and went out into the club.

He could hear the thump of drums from overhead. *Must be nearly time for Sophie to come down.*

He felt a yearning pain in his chest. He wasn't sure whether it was desire or thirst.

God! A tequila would be heaven!

Scrubbing the blackboard he wrote: 'Pizza and chips'. *Shit, it looks a bit bare, maybe 'Pizza Mousecatella' or 'Pizza Infamita'—no! Got to stop playing silly buggers. If they find out...I better leave the back door open in case...*

On his way back to the kitchen he noticed with irritation that the bain-marie trays were still encrusted with last night's curry and spaghetti sauce. Angrily he pulled them out. A wave of greasy stench rose. The power had been left on, and half an inch of nauseous soup was bubbling in the bottom. *Fuck it! I'm not cleaning* that.

He poured in hot water, covered the trays with alfoil and replaced them.

He was suddenly sickened. He walked out, down the passage and into the street.

The sun had gone from the sky and was setting huge and orange behind the freeway. The whole of West Brunswick seemed ablaze with an angry red light; windows shone and glittered, high black clouds raced overhead and a keen wind moaned down the grimy street.

Carl, a little shaken by this apocalyptic scene, hurried back inside, leaving both doors open. *Something bad's going to happen. I know it—I know it.*

He started to wash dishes in a fraught and desultory way.

'Hello, Cookie.'

He turned to see a thin girl with spiky, multi-coloured hair wearing the uniform of the day—gym slip and net stockings. She carried a drink.

'Hi, Carmel, is that for me? Where's Sophie?'

'She's real busy. She told me to give you this.'

'Oh right, thanks. Listen, you tell her to get her arse down here, I want to speak to that young lady.'

'OK, Cookie, I'll tell her.'

Carmel looked at him speculatively.

'What's wrong?'

'Oh, nuthin'.' She giggled and went out.

He took a drink and lit a cigarette. *Shit! The pizzas!* He quickly opened the oven doors. *Just in time!*

Grabbing a tattered cloth, he juggled the trays onto the steel bench. He bent and sniffed, but he could detect only the sweet-sour spice of tomato and cheese, and maybe a slight background of ammonia.

They'll never know what hit 'em. Where's my good knife?

He hunted through the piles of dirty plates till he found his favourite Portuguese knife. It was quite blunt. He set grimly to sharpen it, using the edge of the bench. *It's my own fault. You should never leave your gear around. But this* kitchen—*why didn't Sophie tell me? Why didn't she come down? Why was that Carmel laughing at me?*

Melancholy overcame him; his knife made a mournful scraping. He tested it with his thumb; there was a big nick near the handle. *Shit! There's a good knife fucked—I'll never be able to afford another.*

He cut up the pizza viciously, regarding it dubiously. *Maybe I ought...*

Sophie sidled into the kitchen. She looked at him, her big dark eyes serious.

'Hello, Carl. I can't stay long; Yanni sacked Maria last night and we're real busy.'

'Yeah, now look, Sophie, why didn't you tell me about the kitchen and everything?'

'I'm sorry, but they've been really hassling me upstairs—I would've cleaned up but Laurie said...

Yanni goes: 'I'll get someone in the morning'—I didn't know he...'

Carl saw with surprise that she was going to cry.

'Ah now, Soph.'

He put his arm round her.

'No, don't, Laurie's been really carrying on about you and me—in the passage last night and that. All the girls are laughing...I got to get back!'

'Now listen, Sophie, you've *got* to leave this joint. I walked into Yanni's office before and they were all smacked out of their heads and Laurie really heavied me. This place isn't *safe*. I'm going and you should too.'

'No, I *can't* leave, I told you, I haven't got enough money and I got to leave home.'

'OK, don't worry, I'll get some money and...and I'll take care of you...you could come and...well, when my mother goes, you...'

He was suddenly cautious.

'Look, I'll work it out as long as you...you do...*like* me, don't you?'

'Yeah,' she said slowly, serious. 'I don't really *know* you but.'

Carl heard the thud of heavy boots outside.

'Jesus! There's Laurie and them. Go on Soph, I'll see you later.'

She wiped her eyes with the back of her hand and turned to leave. He was struck again by how young she was.

121

She paused.

'Geez, that pizza looks good—can I have some?'

'Shit, no! Ah…I'll make you one later, OK? Bring me down another drink, huh?'

She shrugged and left. There was a chorus of animal cries outside.

'Hey, come and play with this, little girl!'

'You leave that cook alone! He'll put a bun in your oven!'

Yanni and Laurie entered noisily, followed by the three other bouncers.

'Where's our fuckin' tea, Cookie?'

Yanni was swaying slightly, a sly fatuous grin on his plump face. Laurie stood with legs straddled, his thumbs in his leather pants, his henchmen behind him.

'This kitchen is a fuckin' disgrace—where's our pizza? Hey! That looks *all right*.'

Laurie picked up a big doughy wedge and stuffed it into his mouth, chewing noisily. Carl backed toward the open door. Laurie swallowed.

'Shit, it's fuckin' not bad. About time you cooked something decent.'

They gathered round the trays, scooping up the hot pizza.

'Shit, no olives! Hey, no olives, Cookie.'

'Well, there *wasn't* any.'

'Dumb cunt you Tony. Where's the chips?'

Carl fetched them from the oven and sullenly watched them eat. Yanni had tomato stains down the front of his shirt. He greedily stuffed chips into his mouth.

'Listen, Yanni,' said Carl. 'Who's going to clean up tonight? I'm going to be flat out with this take-away stuff, and yeah! What about my money?'

'Don't you worry,' said Yanni, his voice muffled by greasy chips. 'I'll give you your dough tomorrow *and* a bit extra, but you'll have to clean up tonight—there's a kid coming in tomorrow to give you a hand. All right?'

'Shit, Yanni,' said Carl hopelessly, 'I'll be here till two o'clock in the morning!'

'Now, Cookie, I fuckin' told you before.' Laurie leant into Carl's face again. 'Stop *whingeing*. You do the right thing and stop hassling Yanni. He'll fix you up *tomorrow*. Just you keep them pizzas coming, all right?'

'OK.'

He turned his back on Carl.

'Time to get moving. Tony, you go on the door, Nick on the stairs and we'll go up near the bands, and Tony, don't let Cookie's mate in, you know Mustafa? That little Turkish cunt? Or no! Let him in, I'll fix him right up!'

They left the kitchen, taking the rest of the pizza.

Carl sighed noisily and wiped his face. *How about that! I got away with it! Wow! A new taste sensation. Hang*

123

on! What if Laurie gets sick tonight, or tomorrow…but I'll be gone. Fuck it, I'll worry about it later.

He washed a few more dishes and then carefully scraped and washed the oven trays. Sifting mouse droppings out of the flour with a battered colander he thought of Sophie.

I can't give her pizza, she better have chips. I don't want to make her crook. Poor Sophie—still I better not get carried away there.

He pinched off more yeast, added hot water and sugar and set the jug aside.

Yeah, Sophie…her father looks dangerous. If she moved in with me—in Brunswick! Come on—no— besides, there's Mother. I'll just have to move, a nice flat maybe.

Carl had never lived in a flat. The idea was appealing after years of broken-down terraces.

A box to live in, that's what I need. All clean shiny taps, white paint and berber carpet, maybe some indoor plants and…Sophie, well, perhaps. But the money! Bonds, gas and electricity, moving and proper furniture—Jesus, it would cost a bomb. If I quit here, I'd have to go on the dole—oh no!

He had been on the dole before. It had been a time of humiliation and fear. He had dreaded the fortnightly visit to the dole office and a call from a Social Security Field Officer had thrown him into violent paranoia for weeks. Officialdom of any kind reduced him to stammering idiocy.

I wish I could handle them. Doctors now—if only I could hit a doctor for a pill script instead of relying on guys like Mustafa! But I can't. Them quacks all think I'm a dope fiend.

He felt in his pocket—his mother's pills were still there. He looked at them nestling invitingly in his palm. *No! Not with chips and ovens and that! I couldn't bear a burn tonight.*

He put them away. *Another big drink, that's what I need. That would get me through till nine anyway.*

He wandered round the kitchen restlessly and walked into the dry store.

What else can I put on these pizzas? He found a big tin of pineapple.

Yeah, and ham. But that ham…still, if I really heat it, it won't be so…what else? More cheese—hey! What's this?

He pulled out a half-full bottle of murky liquid labelled 'Chinese Cooking Spirit—Sweet Variety'. *Well, any port in a storm!* He sniggered and took a big swig.

Jesus! Christ! Sickly rawness seared his throat. He coughed violently. *That's awful! Still, maybe with pineapple juice.*

He opened the tin of pineapple chunks and poured the juice into a jug, adding the rest of the bottle.

Ah! Not bad, a new cocktail! 'Marquee Madness'.

He giggled and took another big drink. *Round the world for nothing.*

He paced round the kitchen, sipping. Soon the jug was empty. He set it down with regret and sighed.

The fluorescent lights shone with a kindly radiance and the kitchen suddenly felt familiar and comfortable.

I'll sort of miss this kitchen. Let's face it, I've worked in worse—ah, well.

He started slicing chips again. He was a little clumsy and the knife slipped, giving him a slight nick on his finger. *Whoops! I better watch it, I don't want to leave a finger in the chips!*

He laughed out loud.

He put the chips in the oven, moving with exaggerated care. Even so, he slipped as he was closing the oven door with his knee and smeared his jeans with hot grease.

Shit! My last good pair. I'll have to buy some new clothes, I can't keep wearing the same stuff all the time—Sophie will notice. They care about your clothes, those girls. I could get some of those Italian cotton pants, one of those knitted tops—some loafers—even a double-breasted suit! Yeah, and a striped shirt—that would *make Mother happy.*

He was lost in a sartorial reverie when he heard a shout from the serving area:

'Hey! Any tea?'

He went out, looking at his watch.

126

Two skinny youths waited impatiently in the gloom. Their hair was cropped and slicked above their ears and fell lankly over dark glasses.

'It's not ready yet,' said Carl with irritation. 'Anyway, where's your food tickets?'

'We're from a band.'

'So fuckin' what? You go and get tickets off Tony at the door and come back in half an hour, OK?'

'Shit! This place is the *pits*.'

'Yeah, well don't blame me, pal,' said Carl toughly, 'Yanni makes the rules—no special treatment for bands.'

They retreated, grumbling, into the darkness.

He was struck by a new and disturbing thought. *Sophie! She wouldn't…she couldn't be a* band rat—*no! Anyway she* likes *me, and said so. Take it easy!*

He went to make more pizza.

He mixed the yeast, water, salt and flour in his largest bowl and mixed and kneaded the dough with his hands. He knocked it back, slapping big lumps down hard on the steel bench, enjoying the plasticine feeling. *Just like kinder!* he thought happily, moulding and rolling out wide strips and laying them into oven trays.

Whoops! I should have let it rise. Oh, they'll be right.

Stacking the trays on top of the stove, he lined up his toppings: tomato, onion, pineapple, cheese, *ham. No, I* can't *use that ham.* He sniffed it. *No!* 'When in doubt, throw it out' right.

He picked up the greasy lump and carried it out to the dump-master parked in the passage near the open back door. He looked out. A fine rain slanted down, making the garish club lights pleasantly blurred. Flickering pink neon made the dark street mysterious, a B-movie set. A queue was already forming near the front door and he could see Tony taking money and handing out tickets. Laurie stood massively by, his arms akimbo, towering above the slight kids around him. *Bastard! I hope he gets the runs so bad! I hope he shits those fucking leather pants.*

Carl ducked back inside and lifted the dump-master lid. There was an angry buzz of flies and a terrible stench.

'Christ!'

He threw in the ham; it landed with an unpleasant splash and gurgle. Closing the lid hurriedly, he grimaced.

Jesus! It hasn't been emptied for weeks. Well, it's not my business. But wait! What if I ring up the Health Department on the sly? I'd be doing the right thing and fixing these bastards as well. I'll do it Monday, I will!

Pleased with this Machiavellian scheme, he went back to ponder the pizza problem. Spreading the dough with tomato paste, he paused, nonplussed. *What time is it?*

He looked at his watch; he had to squint to see the red numerals.

128

I must be getting tired already—those kids'll be lined up looking for food soon. Well, I can give 'em chips.

He fetched out the hot chips and dumped the oily load into a bain-marie tray. He tasted one.

Not that bad—salt, they need.

He sprinkled some on and then some more, remembering youthful tastes.

Time for a bit of light! He reached up into a switch box, carefully avoiding a tangle of exposed wires, and pressed a switch. The spotlights flicked on.

The blinding light revealed the squalor of the servery with remorseless clarity.

He hurried back into the kitchen, grabbing a roll of alfoil and switching on the exhaust fans. Using a good half of the roll, he managed to disguise the worst of the muck.

No salad tonight—well they didn't ask for it so fuck 'em. Now, what about these pizzas? I need olives and more ham, and, and…anchovies, yeah. I wonder if that deli round the corner's open—Friday night! Of course it is.

Carl wasn't supposed to leave the kitchen after seven, but in his elevated state he didn't pause. He returned through the passage, peeped through the street door, waited till Laurie's back was turned and slipped out into the night.

*

129

He ran up to Sydney Road and stopped at the corner. He lifted his face to the sky; the soft rain bathed his face. He looked around. Brunswick was almost pretty, like a bad copy of an impressionist painting; the air smelt cool and clean. He felt like running on and on, away from the club forever. Only the thought of his pay stopped him.

The alcohol buzzed pleasantly in his head and he swung confidently up Sydney Road toward the delicatessen.

It was open. Arabic lettering slopped across the window, one side of which was full of dark unfamiliar cuts of meat, the other stacked with tins of chickens and tomatoes. A cedar of Lebanon was painted on the rickety door. He pushed it open and went in, sniffing the rich spicy aromas.

The shop was empty except for a dark middle-aged man waiting quietly behind the counter. A set of worry beads hung from one hand.

'Hi!' said Carl brightly, 'I'm the chef from the club. Yanni's got an account here, hasn't he?'

The man regarded him, frowning.

'Yeah, but he no pay.'

'Well, he said to tell you he'll fix you up tomorrow— we need a few things urgently. OK?'

A plump, tired woman came from the back of the shop and stood by her husband. They had a short conversation in liquid Lebanese Arabic, the man shaking his head and then shrugging.

Carl felt embarrassed and resentful as he always did when hearing a foreign language spoken in front of him. *What are they saying about me?*

'Look,' he said, moving toward the door, 'don't worry about it.'

'All right, what you want?' said the woman. 'Yanni must pay, things very quiet, see?'

She gestured round the shop.

'Oh right, er...large jar of olives, three tins of anchovies and...um, have you got any ham?'

Aren't they Arabs? Arabs don't eat ham, do they? Or is it beef?

'Yeah, we got ham, sure, how much you want?'

'Two kilos, no *three*, and...a carton of Escort cigarettes and...yeah, some of that halva, that bit there.'

Fuck Yanni, I'll get something out of him. I can take most of that ham home too.

'Listen, make that two cartons of Escort, the...the machine's broken down. Right, put it all in a box, will you?'

He roamed round the shop taking a packet of dates here and a box of instant felafel there.

'OK. Yanni'll pay tomorrow.' He grabbed the box and made for the door. 'Shalom!' he cried, and went out.

That didn't sound right—never mind. Shit, I hope Yanni does pay them. They looked a bit...

He looked round again, breathing the damp air. There was a dingy little pub two doors up.

One more little drinkie!

He lunged through the swing door. Two or three old men nursed beers at the other end of the bar.

'A double...ah...Southern Comfort thanks.' *Shit, two bucks left.*

He swallowed the sweet, potent drink and hurried out, round the corner and down to the club, clutching the box under his arm and keeping close to the wall.

The queue was longer and boys and girls were drifting away from the end.

'Fuck waiting round in the rain,' Carl heard as he reached the back door. Two thick-set boys in cut-off T-shirts were arguing with Tony at the front entrance. Laurie stepped out and without a word propelled them down the street, gripping them firmly by the shoulders.

Carl dodged down the passage and into the kitchen, pushing the box under the bench. He sauntered out to the servery, caught his toe in a loose tile and staggered through the door. There was a low round of applause from the few customers waiting patiently holding tickets.

'Any pizza, mister?'

'Pretty soon, kids, how about some chips?'

He fetched a pile of plates and dumped them onto the cold tray. They toppled and slid with a clatter.

'Right, who's first?' he said expansively.

Soon the chips were gone.

'Sorry, kids, that's it for now.'

He felt a little muzzy. *Hell! I better get moving—'feed the starving' and all that.*

He daubed dough with tomato paste and threw on anchovies, olives, ham and cheese with abandon. *Quite artistic this—like action painting.* He stood back and cast mushrooms at random. *Hey, this is fun.*

He threw the trays into the oven, burning himself on the door.

'Shit! Shit! *Shit!*' he yelled, sucking his hand.

He slid the pizza into the oven and held his hand under the cold tap. Too late—a blister was already forming.

He sat down, a little sobered by the pain.

I knew something would…ah shit! What a downer.

He lit a cigarette and sat nursing his hand. Sophie came in briskly.

'Hey, Carl, you got some customers out there, you know.'

'Yeah, I know, I know, it's all coming. I just burnt myself, bugger it.'

She looked at him.

'You all right?'

'Oh yeah, sure, I just…'

He pulled her down onto his knees.

'I just felt a bit pissed off, you know? Jesus, that uniform really suits you.'

He ran his hand up the net stocking.

'No, don't, love. I told you about Laurie and them—someone might come.'

'Bugger Laurie! I'll fix him! I did already,' he said, chortling.

'Oh sure, Carl. Hey, how much have you had to drink?'

'Well, a bit, you know. I found some goodies in the store but I'm all right. Sophie, hey, listen—what you just called me...do you? You know...I mean *I* do.'

'Come on, Carl, I got to go back.'

'Why? Is it busy?'

'No, not really. Not like we thought. Must be the rain—Yanni's shitting himself. He's giving everyone a real hard time—so I'll see you after work, OK? Helen, my girlfriend, you know—she's having a party. You want to come?'

'No, I can't,' he groaned. 'I got to clean up and anyway I have to go home. My mother's staying—shit! I forgot to ring her.'

'OK, Carl, I'll see you later then.'

'No, Sophie, wait! Ring me tomorrow—and we'll talk about you leaving home and that. I'm getting some money soon, a lot really, and we could...well...you know what I mean? You *do,* don't you?'

'Yeah, I guess so. All right, I'll ring you tomorrow afternoon. Take care.'

She laid her cool hand on the back of his neck.

'OK?'

'Oh, Sophie! All right. Yeah, off you go.'

He walked with her to the door and watched her climb the stairs. A boy waiting by the servery followed her sturdy figure with his eyes.

'Bit of a spunk, eh? What d'you reckon?'

'Just shut up, kid! What do *you* want? No pizza for fifteen minutes.'

'All right, all right, Jesus!'

Shit, I better ring Mother—God, I do feel a bit pissed.

His head was starting to pulse. Thundering basses from above shook the air and, with a piercing scream, the night's entertainment commenced.

He picked up the phone and dialled. He had a little difficulty remembering his number. With one hand over his ear:

'Hello, Mother, you all right? Sorry I didn't ring before.'

'I'm fine, dear. I've just had my supper, and I'm sitting down to watch lovely Ronnie Corbett. Are you at work, Carl? I do hope so.'

Jesus! Can't you hear? You deaf old cow! There was a deafening feedback buzz.

'Sorry, Mother, I can't hear a thing. Listen, I'll be late tonight, I have to work back.'

'What I wanted to say to you, dear...'

'No, Mother, I haven't got time. See you tomorrow.'

He put the phone down quickly.

135

Back in the kitchen, he took the pizzas out, sliced them and shook the pieces into the bain-marie. *More chips*…He dragged the bag of potatoes to the bench. On it, in the clutter, he noticed a full glass.

Hey! Good old Soph, she remembered.

Without thinking he took a big drink. His stomach heaved, his eyes blurred and watered and his mouth was full of salty liquid. Clutching the bench, he waited with his head down. *Oh God, I should have had something to eat.*

Picking up his knife, he shakily bent to take a potato from the plastic bag, but the foul smell of preservative was too much. He ran to the toilet and leant weakly against the wall looking down at the murky circle of water in the smeared bowl.

A rush of saliva filled his mouth and he retched and spat. *Oh no, please no.*

In a painful spasm he vomited. He couldn't stand. He slumped to his knees. The stink of his own sickness and old urine met him as he knelt in homage, his arms round the bowl. A solid bolt of vomit spattered into the water, and clear froth gushed from his nose.

He sank back on the hard concrete floor, wiping his mouth with a trembling hand. Surprisingly he felt a bit better. He got to his feet shakily and stumbled back into the kitchen. Through the door he could see more impatient kids waiting for food. *I can't!*

But he did.

For the next half-hour he served pizza, fighting back waves of nausea.

He was sitting trying to make himself start slicing chips when Laurie strode in.

'How's it goin' Cookie? No time for bludging—it looks a bit bare out there.'

'Lay off, Laurie, I'm feeling really crook.'

'What's wrong, you been eating your own grub?'

Carl looked at him with real hatred. *Just you wait!*

'No, I'm serious, I want to go home.'

'No work, no pay, mate. No sickies here—you had it pretty good so far. Do a bit for a change, eh? Yanni's too easy on youse lot. I'll make this joint function yet. Come *on*! Slack-arse.'

He took Carl by the arm and pulled him to his feet, pushing him toward the bench.

'I want to see that servery full. OK?' He turned to go. 'By the way, your fuckin' mate tried to get in again. Tony gave him a big kick in the arse—from you!' Laurie gave a bark of laughter. 'That Mustafa don't like you *at all*. You better watch out goin' home. Yeah, and listen, Cookie, I want to see this kitchen spotless tomorrow. Right?' He left.

Carl sliced potatoes, his impotent rage conquering sickness. *Three, no, four hours to go, then I'm off for good. I'll get some money out of them tonight, even if it's only twenty. I'll get a cab home. Poor bloody Mustafa—they're really bullies.*

His eyes filled with tears.

The next two hours were a blur of toil. He soon ran out of flour and tomato paste and made do with chips, working in a fog of acrid smoke. The hollow boom of the exhaust fans competed with bellowing, shrieking rock'n'roll; his head ached and pounded and his eyes stung unbearably. Luckily, however, his stomach remained quiescent save for an occasional sharp pain in his lower belly. He lost count of the trays of sodden chips tumbled into the servery. At last it was twelve.

He turned off the spotlights, carried in the dirty trays and closed and locked the kitchen door. He squatted for a while, his back against the cool room. Turning, he pressed his hot forehead against the metal.

Shit, I'm too old for this, I really am. I need another holiday—fuck it, I will go on the dole for a while.

He looked around wearily. The kitchen was a shambles of dirty trays and plates, the floor covered with oil. He looked down at himself; his shirt and jeans were stiff with grease. *Well, the sooner I get started...*

He hauled himself to his feet and shut off the fans. He stretched with relief; with the heavy door closed he could hear only a distant thudding from upstairs. He started to clean up.

*

Long after midnight he stood at the sink, drooping with weariness, his arms plunged into lukewarm water, his hands white and pulpy. Occasionally he would nod into sleep, recovering with a start.

Moving mechanically, he finished the dishes and trays and mopped the floor. He wiped down the bench.

That'll do, I can't do any more, fuck Laurie! Just think, after tomorrow, I'll never see them again. Well, anyway, I'm taking all my gear tonight.

He collected his knives and whisks and laid them out on the bench. *My poor beautiful knives.* He ran his thumb along the filleting blade. It shone, the only clean object in the dirty kitchen. He stood like a seedy knight, holding his knife up to the light.

The passage door flew open with a crash. A stocky swarthy man stood swaying in the doorway, his round head thrust forward. His black hair was cropped to the scalp and a white scar ran crookedly down the hairline. His brown face was lumpy and bruised and his mouth hung open, showing broken teeth. A crust of dried blood smeared under his nose. He wore a blue short-sleeved shirt, and his corded arms hung by his sides. Tattered sneakers showed under stained brown trousers.

'Mustafa! What...what are *you* doing here?'

Carl saw that the whites of the Turk's eyes were quite red. Mustafa shuffled forward, breathing noisily, and clung to the bench. Carl backed toward the corner where the bench met the wall.

The Turk spat on the metal.

'I thought you my friend! You cunt like the rest. Where my money? You take pills, no pay, you tell Laurie! You fucking *cunt*!'

'Ah now, Mustafa...look...' Carl, terrified, pressed himself into the corner.

Mustafa came swiftly around the bench.

'No!' Carl shrieked. 'That's *enough*! Leave me alone! *All of you.*'

Suddenly full of rage, trapped, he flung up his hands and pushed Mustafa violently back and fell to his knees sobbing. He looked up, expecting the Turk to fall on him, but instead Mustafa was crouched like a blue-shirted spider at the end of the bench. Carl heard a guttural 'Vay Canina!' The Turk fell slumped heavily forward, out of Carl's sight. There was a sharp *click!* and silence. All he could see was a bare ankle and a sneakered foot.

*

Carl knelt paralysed for a long moment. The music upstairs had stopped. He heard faint voices from

140

outside, the slam of a steel door, and then nothing, absolute quiet.

'Mustafa,' he whispered. He leant forward and touched the bare ankle.

'Mustafa!' Louder.

Carl got to his feet and, his back to the sink, shuffled sideways until he could see the end of the bench and Mustafa lying, his shoulders hunched and his back curved forward. His arms were folded out of sight into his chest and his face turned away so that Carl could see only the nape of his neck.

'Mustafa, come on!' Carl touched the Turk with his toe. *Jesus, he must be pissed, maybe he hit his head.*

Carl bent and pulled a shoulder, but the Turk didn't stir. Carl pulled harder and Mustafa rolled onto his back. Carl leapt away. The Turk's face was twisted, his smashed teeth clenched, his brown eyes open and looking over Carl's shoulder into the fluorescent lights. The pupils seemed wide and soft.

Carl's gaze travelled down Mustafa's body. The brown pants had come open, exposing a black-haired belly. The blue shirt was tucked up in folds. Carl saw near the middle of his chest a small red circle on the cloth—a badge? On it was a...chip of ice? It glittered in the harsh light.

Carl leant forward again urgently. It was the broken blade of his knife. He saw the black handle lying in the Turk's hand.

141

Dave put the phone down quietly and thought for a moment, rubbing his grey curls. Making up his mind, he tip-toed into the bedroom. He could see the red eye of the digital clock: two thirty-five.

'Hey, Junie.' His wife woke with a loud snort.

'Dave! Jesus, look at the time! Come to bed!'

'No, listen, honey, that was Carl on the phone. He's in a bit of strife. I can't make out...he seemed really freaked...I have to go out.'

'What! Dave, you just *dare*.'

'No, I have to go.'

'All right, you *go* then, if you're going out boozing with that little creep...well just...Jesus!'

'Ah, come on, baby.'

'No, go on, piss off, and you sleep in the boys' room when you come back. I'll speak to you tomorrow!'

She turned over, plunging angrily in the bedclothes. Dave hesitated and went out.

It was very dark outside; a light rain was falling. As he sat to put on his boots, his cat curled around his leg. He stroked it absently. Shrugging, he stood, limped to his car and drove off down into Brunswick.

Turning into Basilisk Street, he parked outside the club. The neon sign was off and the street was quiet and deserted. An occasional car swished past in Sydney Road. Rain drifted slowly in the headlights. Dave switched them off, got out and tried the big steel entrance. It was locked. What did he say? 'Passage door.' He walked back and found another smaller door; it swung open at his touch. The darkness inside was impenetrable. Dave marched heavily forward, his hands out, feeling his way.

'Carl! Carl! Where are you?' There was a gasp and he felt the draft of movement. A hand clutched his arm.

'Ah, Dave! I knew you'd come.'

Dave felt Carl's thin body against him. It was shaking.

'Jesus, old mate, what have they been doing to you?' He patted Carl awkwardly on the shoulder. 'Look, let's have some light.'

'Wait,' said Carl. 'Come in.' A door closed behind them and Dave heard Carl fumbling at the wall. The lights flicked on. Dave looked around.

'What *is* going on?'

Carl's face was yellow and streaked with tears, his hands twitching and fluttering.

'Dave, Dave, look in the coolroom!' Carl clumsily unlocked the heavy metal door. 'Go on. Underneath the potatoes.'

Carl heard the potato bags being shifted. There was a short silence, then:

'Shit! Who's this?' Dave came out. 'Jesus Christ, Carl! This guy's dead!'

'I know! I know! It's Mustafa,' Carl cried. 'I told you about him.'

'Yeah, yeah, but who did it? He's been *stabbed*!'

'Dave, I did, I didn't mean to, I swear to God. He had a go at me. He was going to...I don't know...I pushed him away. I must have had my knife in my hand...he just fell over! What are we going to do!?'

'Well, I don't know,' said Dave slowly. 'I suppose we better tell the cops...I mean it was self-defence or an accident, wasn't it? They won't...you put him in there, did you?'

'Yes, yes, I had to hide him so I could *think*. Dave, look, I *can't* tell the cops. Listen...look, I know this sounds...but *Mother*...she's sick. I'll never get any money...I *couldn't* go to jail. Dave, I couldn't go

144

through a *trial* and everything...I *couldn't*...I'll...
I'd *kill* myself...ah shit, everything's been really good
today...and now this!' Carl was crying again. 'Dave,
we'll have to hide him or something, *please!* Dave, help
me.'

'Jesus, mate.' said Dave. 'I've got a wife and
kids...look, you'll be...they...'

'Dave, I can't tell the cops—what if they found out
about the *dope*! I couldn't go to jail, I *would* die...Dave,
you always *said* that...Dave, you're my friend!'

Dave looked away from Carl's face, ugly in its
terror.

'Well, I suppose we could take him up the hills or
something.'

'Yes, Dave! That's right, in the bush! Away from
here. Ah! I knew you'd help me!'

'Look, Carl, do you swear you...OK, OK, never
mind, let me think. Go and sit down and calm down!'

Carl went and sat like an errant schoolboy, his head
bowed. Occasionally he glanced at Dave who stood
drumming his big fingers on the steel bench top.

'Did anyone see him come in? How did he get in?
What I mean is, was there any *witnesses?*'

'No, Dave, no, he came through the back door
just when they were closing. No one was round, that's
why...the cops'll...they wouldn't believe I didn't mean
it. They'd think it was a fight about *drugs*—how could
I...'

'OK, OK. Well, we'll have to get him into my car, that's the first thing. And then we'll take him out into the bush and I suppose we bury him...hey! Wait a minute.'

'What? It's the only thing to do, Dave, look...'

'No, shut up!...I just thought...I dug a fuckin' *grave* today. Jesus! *Of course.* Listen Carl, with a bit of luck, you're right.' And Dave explained.

Carl listened puzzled.

'But won't someone...? No, let's take him into the bush.'

'No fear,' said Dave. 'They find some stiff in the bush every week. We couldn't take him far enough tonight to be sure. This way no one will ever find him.' He slapped his hand on the bench. 'Come on, let's get him out.'

'Oh, Dave, I don't think I...'

'Come on, Carl, you're going to have to help me with this—look at me.' He took Carl's head in his hands and shook him gently. 'Now, come on, mate, trust me, all right?'

Dave went back into the coolroom. Carl heard dragging noises, he turned his head quickly away, seeing the blue shirt out of the corner of his eye.

'First we better get this blade out of him, just in case he ever...Now, you wait here, Carl, I'll be back in a tick.'

'No, Dave! Where are you going?'

'I'm just getting my pliers.'

146

'Oh, Jesus!' Carl buried his face in his hands.

Soon Dave was back. He bent down.

'Christ, you got him right between the sixth and seventh ribs. Didn't you realize...didn't you feel anything?'

'No, no, I didn't *know*. Dave, how can you...'

'I used to be a medical student, you know that. I've seen more stiffs...OK now.' Carl heard a sucking noise.

'Oh Dave! I...'

'If you want to chuck, do it now.'

'No, I'll be all right. It will be OK, won't it, Dave?'

'Yeah, sure. Now where's the handle...Jesus, he hardly bled at all—he must have died, *bang!* just like that. Now, we better take him out. What can we cover him up with?'

'There's some old rice sacks in the passage,' Carl said.

'Now you're thinking. Good boy. Go and get 'em. This knife now, I'll put it...I'll think of somewhere later.'

Carl fetched the rice bags and Dave wrapped the corpse and bound the bundle with trussing twine.

'OK, Carl, now you take the legs.'

They lifted the body. There was a loud gurgle.

'Christ! Dave, he's alive!' Carl dropped his end.

'All right mate, that's just fluids inside him. Look out, I'll take him.'

'Oh God!' Carl turned away helplessly.

Dave stopped, and with a huge effort slung the long bundle onto his shoulder.

'Now go and keep a lookout.'

Carl stumbled out through the passage. The street was empty. He strained his eyes wildly up and down. He felt a nudge in his back; it was the shrouded head. He shrieked,

'Dave, don't! Jesus!'

'Shut up, go and open the car...no, the *boot*. Jesus, hurry up, he's bloody heavy.'

'OK.' Dave dropped his burden in the boot with a groan.

'Shit, my *leg*—you better hope it holds out! Right now, go and lock the door and we'll be off.'

Dave started the car, the old engine roaring in the silent street. They turned left in Sydney Road and drove sedately north.

'Look, Carl, do up your seat belt, for Christ's sake. We don't want the cops stopping us.'

Carl fumbled for the strap. He saw Dave's face in the glow of the rain-blurred lights. It was relaxed. His big hands lay lightly on the steering wheel.

'Dave, you don't know what...Dave, I'll never forget this...'

'All right, all right. Listen, we're not even halfway getting this done, take it easy. Just keep your head, OK?'

'Yeah, Dave, I will! I promise, I just wish...'

*

Soon they reached Bell Street and turned right, driving east for five minutes. Dave cut the lights and ignition and they coasted to a stop under a big old gum. He flicked the lights once and Carl saw a great set of wrought iron gates. Across the top in curled lettering he read 'Coburg Cemetery'.

'OK, now you sit tight for a minute.' Dave opened the car door.

'Dave, please!'

But he was gone. Carl heard the groan of iron hinges and then nothing but heavy drops of rain on the car roof.

Dave opened the car door and got in again.

'So far, no worries. Bluey, that's the caretaker, he's out like a light. He wouldn't wake up if we put old Mustafa in his bed! Now we go round to the side gate. That's where you're really going to have to help me, mate. We're going to have to carry him a fair way. Can you do it?'

'Yeah, I guess so. I'll have to. Dave, you're...you're *enjoying* this.'

'Ah, come on! Well yeah...in a way. Look...never mind, let's go!'

They drove slowly round the cemetery fence. Iron railings flicked past in the lights.

'Thank Christ for this rain, there'll be no bastard wandering round. I'll park behind those bushes.'

Dave slid the car between two large grevilleas.
Thorns whipped the windows. He cut the motor.

'Now, we need a torch. What else? A *tyre lever*, yeah.'

'What for?'

'You'll see. And a shovel. I'll have to go to the shed for that...we better get him up there first.'

They got out and Dave opened the boot.

'Right. Up you come!'

And he heaved the long bundle out and laid it on the grass. Carl stared wildly round. There was a street light nearby, but they were hidden by the bushes.

'OK,' Dave muttered, 'Torch, tyre lever—stick it in your belt—now, where's the key? Front gate, shed, office, *side gate*. Right, beauty!'

'Oh, Dave, hurry up, someone might come!'

'Easy now, mate.'

Dave unlocked the gate. It swung open with a screech of rusty iron.

'We don't use this much. Now, can you take the feet? We'll take it slow and easy. OK?'

Carl picked up his end. The bundle folded flaccidly. He felt the thick ankles through the sacking. Dave held the shoulders and backed through the gate.

'All right, put him down. This is no good. I can't see where I'm going. I better lock up again, anyway. Now let me think...' Dave said. 'I better carry him like a roll of carpet—like this.' He crouched, clutching the bundle to his back, holding it over his shoulders. 'Now when I get up, you take the legs, but don't lift them too high. OK?'

Dave rose grunting. Carl took the legs and they started forward, Dave's boots crunching heavily into the gravel path.

Away from the street lights it was very dark. Carl felt rather than saw the loom of stone monuments. The rain pelted down, hissing in the blackness.

'Why's he so *limp*?' Carl cried, stumbling. 'I thought they went stiff!'

'Jesus, keep your voice down—they don't get that way for hours yet, thank Christ.'

On they trudged. Carl was lost in misery, his panic replaced by an immense fatigue.

They were climbing a slight hill. The graves were flatter here and the path much narrower. Carl tripped and fell, barking his shins painfully on a marble slab. Dave was pulled backwards, dropping the bundle.

'Shit! Watch it, Carl. Where are we?' He flashed the torch quickly onto the slab. '"Di Farenza". Thank Christ. We're in the Italian section. Not far now...just hang on.'

He sat rubbing his leg.

'What's wrong?' Carl's voice rose in the darkness.

'Ah, it's my fucking leg.'

'Oh, Dave, you can't stop now!'

'All right, all right, I'm OK, come on!'

They laboured on, Carl following blindly as Dave picked his way unerringly around graves and through rank, wet grass.

'This is it, mate.' Dave let the bundle slump. Carl knelt panting in the mud.

'Give us a hand and we'll put him behind this stone. I'll get a shovel from the shed—you stay here and don't move!'

'Dave, let me come! I don't want to stay here with...'

'Don't worry, he can't hurt you now.'

They rolled the body behind a long low monument and Carl crouched over it miserably. Dave disappeared again.

Carl, his eyes straining in the dark, crawled around on his knees, his hands outstretched. He found a heap of gravel and mud. There was a rattle of falling stones. One hand slid down a long edge of slick clay and then into emptiness. *The grave.*

He recoiled.

He was kneeling, his body bowed, his knees deep in the mud. *Please! If you get me out of this, I'll never...I'll believe in you.* He pitched forward onto the clay heap.

His mind slid away. There was a high singing in his ears. Great shining yellow circles turned, wheeled and receded in the velvet black. His limbs jerked and shuddered, ploughing the mud. Then he lay still.

'Carl, Carl! Where the fuck are you?'

Carl felt comfortable. His cheek nestled in the soft wet earth. His limbs felt blissfully languorous, his mind drifted lazily. *I'm in the graveyard. Why?*

A blinding light flashed in his face. He sat up gasping.

'You all right?' said Dave.

'Yeah, sure. I just...I don't know,' Carl said. *What happened to me?*

He felt he had lost some part of himself. His mouth felt sore. He had bitten his tongue.

'Now listen,' said Dave urgently, 'you'll have to hold the torch, right? And when I tell you, flash it on and off, but do it *quick*, OK? And hold it into the hole, it's over here. Got that?'

'Oh yeah, right.'

'Come on then.'

Carl wandered round in the dark.

'Over *here*,' called Dave.

'OK, OK.' Carl felt for the edge of the hole. He touched Dave's head.

'Right now,' said Dave. 'A quick flick...no! Jesus! Into the *grave*—Christ! Give it to me!' Dave climbed down, his boots thudding into the props. He reached up.

'Here, take it, I've wrapped my shirt around so you can leave it on.'

Carl held the torch, its light channelled by Dave's T-shirt. He saw his friend's naked back stooping in the

153

narrow shaft. He heard the scrape of a shovel. Gravel sprayed out. Soon there were hollow thuds; metal on wood.

'Jesus, it's wet down here. Give me more light...hold it *down*...right...here it is.' Dave straightened up. Carl held the torch well down. He saw a black wooden rectangle smeared with clay. It looked like an old split door. *Open Sesame.*

'OK,' Dave said, 'give us that tyre iron.'

'What are you going to do?'

'I'm going to take this lid off and give Maria a bit of company!'

'But...OK, whatever you reckon, Dave.'

Carl felt washed by trust. He looked at Dave's face raised to his. Dave was grinning through his grey beard. His eyes shone like an excited cat's in the torchlight.

'Give us that iron now, and hold the light well down.'

Carl pulled the tyre lever from his belt, gave it to Dave, and lay on his stomach, his arm stretched into the grave.

Dave bent grunting with effort. The muscles in his shoulders rose. There was an incredibly loud splintering crash.

'Jesus! Lights out! Now shush!'

Carl lay, his arm pointing down, the heavy torch in his rigid fingers. He raised his head from the dirt. He could hear only the drip and splash of the rain. They waited.

'OK, let's see.'

Carl flicked on the torch. Dave was balanced on the lowest row of props, his boots jammed into the clay. The coffin lid was split down the middle and both sides lay loose. Dave pulled them up and Carl saw a long yellow-grey tattered shape. The torchlight wavered.

'Hold it steady!'

Dave bent again and ripped this cloth from end to end with the claw of the tyre lever. The rotten shroud came easily away.

'Oh Jesus!'

First he saw a mask of brown ragged parchment resting on a mat of grey hair. The empty eye sockets looked quietly into Carl's mind. Gold teeth gleamed in the lipless mouth. Long pitted bones crossed the ribcage, disappearing into a slurry of green and black. Thick grey masses fell from the raised thighs. The knees were naked cord and bone. Carl dropped the torch. It went out.

'Holy Christ! I didn't think it would...you all right, Carl?'

It wasn't real, *it wasn't* real.

Carl fixed his reeling mind and held it.

'Yeah, I think so...'

'Don't worry about the light now, I'm going to have to make room for the *other*. Go away for a while if you want to.' Dave's voice shook a little.

'No,' said Carl, 'I'm OK.'

'Right then.'

And Carl heard Dave jump down into *that*! He heard the heavy stamping of Dave's boots. There was a sound as of green branches splintering and breaking. He smelt a strange odour—like fungus and tar.

'All right, Carl, go and get him.'

'Dave, I don't think I...'

'Go and fucking get him *now*!'

Carl crawled around in the dark till he found the long, still bundle. The wrapping had come away from the shoulders but he grasped them anyway. He heaved, but his strength was totally gone.

'Dave! I can't lift him!'

'Well, fucking *roll* him then, hurry up!'

Carl shuffled forward on his knees rolling the bundle up the mound of clay.

'Right, let him slip, I've got him.'

Carl felt Dave take the weight. There were thuds, a heavy slithering and the choc! choc! of metal on wood.

Dave sighed loudly.

'Right, help me out...hang on, watch out for the shovel.' It clanged onto gravel.

'Where's your hands?'

Carl clasped Dave's forearms, feeling the big muscles flex. With a heave he was out. He stood up slowly. Carl could see him faintly against the sky; the rain had stopped and a star or two hid in the clouds.

Dave stooped again, picked up the shovel and threw gravel rattling into the grave.

Suddenly Carl bent, feverishly scooping up the dirt with his hands and flinging it in.

'Hey, take it easy, Carl, we only want about six inches—that'll do, that's it. Let's get out of here! Have we got everything? I'll leave the shovel here, I got to use it tomorrow.'

'Dave, where's the torch?'

'Don't worry about the torch,' Dave said grimly, 'it landed in *that* and I wasn't going to pick it out.'

'Oh, Dave! Wasn't it...'

'Yeah, don't think about it. But I'll tell you what, I'm getting rid of these boots!'

He knelt and took them off, throwing them violently into the darkness.

'Phew! Right, give us your hand, let's go.'

Carl let himself be led like a child through the dim labyrinth. He could see a little more now—huge trees rose against the greying east. He heard the first birds.

'Come on, mate,' Dave said gently. 'It's getting light.'

They reached the gate in silence. Dave unlocked it, then:

'Dave, what was that green stuff?' Carl's tone was level, enquiring.

'What green...oh yeah. Fuck, I don't know. *Mould*, I guess. Jesus! They ought to *burn* them. I thought it would be just *bones*. I'm giving this job away...ah, bugger it, it's over now. Or nearly. Eleven tomorrow, there's the funeral and I'll fill it in and that's *it*.'

'Dave, it was a woman, wasn't it?'

'Look, Carl, just shut up about it, all right? I *told* you, that's it.' They got into the car.

'Dave, where's your shirt?'

Dave hunched his big shoulders.

'With the fucking torch...Look, I'll drop you home, OK?'

They drove south into Brunswick. Carl was silent now and when Dave glanced at him he was staring straight ahead, his face lined and haggard in the pale light. There was something uncharacteristic, unnatural in his stillness.

The car pulled up outside Carl's house.

'Carl, you OK? You got some pills? I know you don't sleep too good...and after that!'

'No, I'm fine,' Carl said slowly, his voice without colour. 'Something happened to me back there when you were away. I feel different than I ever felt before...yeah, I'm OK.'

He turned, looking Dave straight in the eyes. For some reason Dave wanted to look away, but he couldn't.

'You know why we had to do all that, don't you?'

'Yeah, sure,' Dave said. 'You couldn't tell the cops, they wouldn't believe it was an accident...you said.'

'Yeah, there was all that, but not just that. My mother. I told you she's left me all that money. Anything like this, she'd cut me out—I know her.'

'Ah, come on, she couldn't be as bad as all that. It wasn't your fault. Anyway, *money*. Shit!'

Dave felt uncomfortable, queerly embarrassed.

'It's OK for you,' Carl said in the toneless voice. 'You're happy, I'm not. I never have been, ever. Maybe I never will be, but that money'll give me a chance. You can't understand that, I know. You probably think I'm a real creep. Well, I can't help that.'

'Ah well, yeah, all right mate. Look, you better get to bed, I got to get home. June'll kill me...sorry...I mean...' Dave was puzzled, even a little scared, by Carl's manner.

'Yeah, June,' said Carl slowly. 'You won't tell her anything about this, will you? Or anyone else.'

'No, of course not. June wouldn't understand. And as for anyone...I'm an *accessory* now.'

'Yeah, that's right, you are. Ha!' Carl gave a short bark of laughter. He looked around at the peeling weatherboard cottages, the dusty ti-trees, shabby in the dawn light. 'I'd do anything to get out of here. I don't want to live like this any more. I'm too old.'

'OK, mate, bedtime!' said Dave. 'I'll ring you tomorrow, after...you know. Where will you be?'

'I don't know,' said Carl, opening the car door. 'I have to go to work for a while, in the afternoon.'

'Shit? Will you be able to handle that?'

'Yes, I will,' Carl said flatly. He turned and went up his front path.

Dave stared at his back.

'Jesus!' he said to himself. 'He must be in shock or something.'

He started the car as quietly as he could and drove home.

*

After an uncomfortable few hours on the spare bunk in the boys' room, Dave woke to the sound of clashing pots in the kitchen. The boys were up and he could hear them noisily enjoying their breakfast, their shrill conversation punctuated by June's hoarse cries of admonition.

He got up and pulled on his jeans. As always in the morning, his knee throbbed and ached. This time, however, there was a sharper, gnawing pain. He bent and rubbed his leg hard, digging his fingers into the wasted muscle below the joint. The hurt eased a little and he straightened with difficulty and limped heavily into the kitchen.

June was washing up, her back rigid and her face averted.

'Hiya, Dad, how come you slept in our room? You having a fight with Mum, are ya?'

'Morning chaps! I don't know, did I? Am I?' Dave said, addressing June's back.

'Yes, we bloody well are!' she said, turning angrily. 'Do you know what time you got home? You woke Leon and it took me *hours* to get him down again. Didn't you bloody hear him?'

'No, hon. I was pretty tired and that, I tried to be quiet.'

'What the hell were you *doing*, anyway?' She looked at him narrowly. 'Look at you! You're covered in…what is it? *Mud*. Look, it's even in your hair, and you stink. I can smell you from here.'

'Daddy smells!' The boys were delighted. 'Daddy stinks!'

June turned on them.

'Get outside, you boys, you're no better. Go on, *out*. Bloody males!'

The boys left, chastened.

'Now, Dave, I want to hear what you were doing last night. Out boozing with Carl, were you?'

'No, Babe, I swear I didn't have one drink. Look, Carl was in a bit of trouble and I had to help him out, that's all.'

'What *kind* of trouble? Little prick, he's old enough to look after himself. What are you? His bloody dad? Come on, tell me, what kind of trouble? I *am* your wife, you know.'

161

Dave was too tired to think of a convincing lie. He stood stolidly, looking down.

'I can't tell you. I promised...Look, I've got to have a shower, I have to go to work soon.'

'You stay right here, Dave. I'm sick to death of this male bonding business. Bloody men, they stick together like...like maggots! If I was out all night, you'd want to know where I was, wouldn't you? So spill it!'

'June, I *can't*, please, I promised. Look, I got to go to work.' He trod lopsidedly into the bathroom.

'Well, I might just not be here when you get back!'

'Fuck! Fuck!' he said, sitting on the toilet and peeling off his clay-smeared jeans.

He stood under the shower, frowning worriedly, his mild eyes looking through the falling water. His great torso and thick arms sat oddly on his short legs, the left twisted and withered.

After the shower he felt better; his knee felt looser and ached less. He went to dress. Pulling on clean jeans, T-shirt and socks, he looked round for his boots.

'Shit!' He remembered...suddenly the previous night became real. 'I *can't* tell June, and that's that.'

Putting on his old sneakers, he went out to look for her.

She was in the big back yard feeding the fowls. The boys played quietly in their tree house and Leon slept in his cot on the back porch. The air was heavy and warm.

'Well, I've got to go, Junie.'

'You still won't tell me, huh? All right. You be back by one-thirty. I'm going out.'

'Yeah, sure, OK, hon. Look...'

'You want to know where I'm going?' she said fiercely. 'I'll *tell* you. I'm going to the Women's Refuge Collective meeting, and we'll be talking about your kind of crap, you can bet your life on that!'

'God, June! You can't talk about our private life in *public*. Jesus!'

'Oh yes I can, you creep. This is a *political* issue. It's about time we women got together to stop this male bonding bullshit. Now get out of my sight!' She turned back to the chooks, flinging feed at them. They clucked with alarm.

'Daddy's in the shit!' The boys hung grinning from the tree house like gibbons.

'Shut up!' Dave shouted, and they fell silent, surprised; he was usually so good natured. He strode out to the car, swinging his bad leg.

*

Driving to the cemetery, he realized that he had left without breakfast. Stopping in Sydney Road, he went into a hamburger shop filled with the Saturday morning crowd. While he waited for a steak sandwich, he watched the Greek couple behind the counter working together—the wife deftly slicing onions and the husband

163

flipping hamburgers and fried eggs on and off the hot plate. He thought of June and sighed.

Still eating his sandwich, he pulled up at the cemetery gate—it was open. He drove in, stopping outside the caretaker's cottage.

'Hey, Blue! You there?'

Bluey came out blinking in the hot sunlight. He looked much as usual—no worse for his debauch.

'How you feeling, Bluey?'

'Not too bad, Dave, old mate—bit of a head but. How's the gun gravedigger this morning? By Jeez, you look a bit fucked yourself, you been on the piss too?'

'No, mate, my leg's playing up a bit, that's all. You heard from the undertakers? Who is it?'

'Murphy's,' said Bluey. 'They're gonna be a bit late, eleven twenty or so.'

'Murphy's? How come? It's an Italian job, isn't it? What about the Casteluccis?'

'Ain't you heard? They're in strife with the tax boys. They've had to close down for a bit. By Christ, they're sly buggers, them Casteluccis...couple of years ago, before your time it was, they used to get up to some tricks, by Jeez they did!' Bluey cackled. 'They'd have them stiffs stacked up in them holes like...like fuckin' *egg boxes*! They was selling plots three and four times over! Them was the days!'

'Yeah, I heard,' said Dave. 'Look, Blue, here's your spare keys.'

'Ta, Dave. Listen, mate, thanks for locking up and that. I couldn't fuckin' scratch last night…I'll tell you what, it ain't my job, but I'll help you fill her in. How about that?'

'No, Blue, you don't have to…'

'No, mate, fair's fuckin' fair. You want a cuppa tea or a heartstarter maybe?' Bluey winked. 'I am, by Christ.' He turned back into the cottage.

'No thanks, Blue. Don't forget you'll have to bring the covers and straps.'

'Yeah, no worries, see you in a while.'

Dave drove down the hill, parked and looked at his watch—ten to. He got out and limped up the slope as quickly as he could. The sun was very bright now. Granite and marble gleamed in the rain-washed air and water droplets sparkled on every leaf.

Soon he reached the open grave. He looked about carefully. His shovel lay on the gravel path, the blade spotted with rust. There was a confusion of footprints and the mud was churned and furrowed around the clay heap where Carl had lain.

He hesitated and then looked into the hole. It looked all right except for one edge which was broken away. He straightened it with the shovel.

Then he cast around, looking for his boots, and found them lying some distance away. Flies buzzed around thick dark stains on the soles. He turned away in disgust, fetched his shovel and buried them hurriedly.

Returning to the grave, he started to smooth the gravel path, filling in the deeper footprints.

A big grey American car drew smoothly up at the bottom of the hill. Dave could see chaste lettering on the door: 'Murphy's—The Grief Managers'. A spare, balding, middle-aged man got out. He was dressed in a black coat and striped trousers.

'How you goin', mate? Dave, isn't it?' The undertaker was puffing slightly from the short climb.

'Yeah,' said Dave. 'How you doin'?'

'Buggers are late as usual. Wog funerals—I don't know. Still, they really spend. Wait till you see the casket. It looks like a space capsule! Imported American, it is.'

'That so,' said Dave indifferently.

'Yep. Ah…bit untidy, mate. Don't you reckon?'

The undertaker was looking at the grave. 'Better clean it up a bit—you'll have to take those props out anyway. Where's the covers?'

'Bluey's bringing them up. Here he comes now.'

Dave climbed down into the hole, knocking out the props as he went. He paused as he reached the final set, then planted his feet firmly onto the bottom of the grave. He moved his feet cautiously. He could feel the edges of the coffin boards through the thin covering of gravel.

He threw the props out. Bluey's wattled face appeared.

'Need a hand, mate?'

'No, I'm right.'

He pulled himself up.

Dave and Bluey spread green tarpaulins over the pile of clay and Dave started to smooth the gravel again.

'Jeez, what was you and Mick doing' up here yesterday, dancing or what? I thought you was the *gun*. You left a bit of a fuckin' mess.'

As Dave filled in the footmarks, he recognized the prints of Carl's ripple soles.

'Off you go, Blue' he said, 'they'll be here soon. You'll have to meet them and fill in the book.'

'Come on, Blue,' said the undertaker. 'I'll give you a lift.' He looked at his watch. 'They should be here in seven minutes exactly.'

Dave laid stout woven straps across the hole—these were to lower the coffin—and wiped clay from the headstone. Soon he saw a long line of cars slowing at the cemetery gates and then winding down towards him.

First the undertaker's car drew up with Bluey in the passenger seat like a debauched Charon. Then came the hearse, low and sleek, its roof heaped with wreaths.

Dave could see that the casket did indeed resemble a piece of space hardware; round nosed and streamlined, it gleamed dully under more flowers.

The following line of cars bunched up and there was the usual unedifying, confused competition for parking spaces in the narrow driveway.

Black-clad mourners gathered as the casket was slid from the hearse. The procession, headed by a priest, formed and mounted the slope—the undertaker, walking to one side, directed the straggling line with restrained gestures. The heavy metal box bobbed and swayed as its bearers shuffled awkwardly up through the crowded graves.

Dave withdrew discreetly, taking his shovel, and sat behind a large monument some distance away. Bluey joined him.

'Jeez, I'm *rapt* in wog funerals,' Bluey said gleefully. 'You watch, there'll be some sheila trying to throw herself in—they'll be screaming and carrying on—beauty! Them wogs, if you cut their throats and took off their hands, by Christ! They'd talk with their feet!'

'Shut up, Blue,' said Dave. 'Christ, have some... Jesus, I wish it was fuckin' over.'

'What's up you? You're gettin' paid, aren't you? Time and a half after twelve...you sign on, didya?'

'Shit! No, I forgot...come on, come on!' Dave said, watching the priest. 'Get on with it.'

'We'll get a good tip with Murphy's, too,' Bluey continued, 'not like them Casteluccis. You know they charge the family ten bucks for gravediggers and give us one. Wog cunts!'

'Who is it?' Dave nodded toward the funeral. 'The husband, is it?'

'Nah, must be the daughter, judging by the plate. Funny but, usually the old man goes first, you noticed?'

'Yeah, yeah.'

The funeral ground on. Despite what Bluey had said, there was little emotion shown except by a bowed elderly man standing by the priest's side. Occasionally he would wipe his face or turn his head away sharply in a gesture of grief. The others stood black and stolid in the hot sun.

Dave looked on with guilt and pity. *Sorry, old man—we had to do it.*

At last the service was over and the casket was lowered. Dave stood impatiently.

'Go on, piss off!' he muttered. Mourners drifted round uncertainly, as they always did, talking quietly and greeting one another. The old man was helped down the hill by the priest. One by one the cars drove away.

The undertaker came over, smiling genially.

'Well, that went very nice. Quiet like. You can never tell with wops, you know. These were Sicilians but.

They're different—don't carry on. Here you are, boys, have a drink.'

He handed Bluey some notes.

'Thanks very much, Mr Murphy,' said Bluey obsequiously, 'glad it went good. See you next time.'

*

The undertaker left and Dave hurried to the grave.

'What's up, you? What's your rush?' said Bluey. 'You're gettin' overtime, remember. Besides, there's someone left.'

'Where?' said Dave, looking round.

'Over there, behind the trees.'

It was a thin figure, neatly dressed in a blue shirt and narrow tie, its white-blond hair lambent against the dark green cypresses.

'Jesus!' Dave whispered to himself, 'It's *Carl*.'

'Who is it?' asked Bluey puzzled. 'You know him?'

'No! Come on, let's start.'

'You sure you don't know him? He's not from the Trust is he? He don't look like no wog relation to me!'

'No, Bluey, I *told* you.'

'From the fuckin' union then,' said Bluey suspiciously. 'You tell them to stay off me back!'

'*No*, Blue. Come *on*.'

Dave threw a shovelful of clay into the grave. There was a loud, hollow, metallic thud. Swinging his torso, his feet planted firmly, he worked furiously, Bluey throwing in the occasional clod.

'Want to do it all yourself, do you? All right, Dave, suit yourself. I'm off for a beer. Here's *your* whack.' He handed Dave a crumpled note.

'Yeah, OK, Blue. Sorry, mate. Sometimes this job gets me down.'

'Yeah, well, you haven't bin here that long, have ya? But listen, you sure that bloke's not a boss? Even if he was, you don't have to bust a gut, you know.'

'No, I told you. I don't know him. Go and have a beer and I'll see you after I sign off.'

Bluey shouldered his pick and left, dodging nimbly between the low slabs.

Dave looked round again. Carl hadn't moved. Dave was too far away to see his eyes but he felt Carl's steady gaze. Dave started to limp towards him, stopped uncertainly, then turned and laboured on.

Sweat ran down his back, soaking his T-shirt. He swung his body violently, the shovel clunking into the clay and ringing on the gravel. Pain bit into his knee...the hole filled with great wet clods.

Working steadily, it usually took two men about an hour to fill a shallow grave like this. It took Dave half an hour.

He finished, flinging down the shovel. Leaning forward gasping, he rested his hands on his knees, his head hanging. Sweat stung his eyes...Wearily he straightened and started to heap wreaths on the low mound. He heard a soft footfall: it was Carl.

'Carl! What are you *doing* here? Jesus, mate, you gave me a shock. Sorry I didn't come over before, but I told Bluey I didn't know you. I thought...' Dave trailed off.

Carl stood looking at the grave, his face pale, dark smudges under his green eyes. His thin body seemed braced against an invisible force. Dave noticed with a queer feeling of pity that his hair was neatly combed. His narrow tie was tucked into the waistband of his grey trousers. His long-sleeved shirt was crisply ironed, with a pin through the collar. He looked like a worn and ageing schoolboy. Dave remembered with pain how good-looking he had been.

Carl turned his head and looked at Dave.

'I wanted to see it finished, that's all.' His voice was toneless.

'Yeah, of course you did. Well, it *is*. You've got no worries now, have you? I mean…I didn't tell June. She…'

'She wouldn't believe you anyway.' Carl smiled, showing his bad teeth.

'No, that's right, who would,' said Dave, fumbling with the wreaths.

'Dave…why weren't you *surprised* last night?'

'What do you mean, surprised? Well, yeah, I suppose I wasn't…I don't know why. You…I just *dunno*.' Dave stood. 'Look, just forget about it if you can. What are you doing this arvo? Come back to my place and have a few beers. We'll listen to some Bird and get a bit pissed and…June's going to some feminist thing, she'll be out all afternoon.'

172

'No, I have to go to work. It'd look funny if I didn't. And then I have to look after Mother.'

'Well then, I'll drive you down...just hang on till I finish.'

Carl turned away and started down the slope.

'No, Dave. I can't see you any more...you should know that.'

'Carl! Wait!' Dave started after him. 'Carl!'

Dave, his eyes on Carl's back, slipped in the loose sloping gravel and fell heavily on to his bad leg. His knee twisted agonizingly. He tried to get up.

'Carl!'

Carl didn't look back.

*

Carl caught the tram to work, down Sydney Road. It was one of the new orange type with folding hydraulic doors. They hissed closed behind him.

The tram was crowded with shoppers going home with laden baskets. He stood for a long moment in front of the conductor seated behind his change machine.

'Come on, mate!'

At last Carl took a dollar from his pocket. It was his last...He handed over the coin, got a ticket, pushed his way through the crowd and sat down ahead of a heavily laden Greek lady. He sat, looking straight ahead, oblivious to her angry mutterings.

The tram made its jerky way down Sydney Road. The doors swished and thumped. It was very hot. The crowd swayed and lurched.

He glanced out of the window to his right. The bright sun outside threatened him like an interrogator's spotlight. He looked away to his left but the packed tram pressed on him like a suffocating blanket...he found it hard to breathe. He felt like tearing open his tight collar. A dull pain grew in his chest. Concentrating hard, he held his hands steady in his lap and his head rigid.

Stop! Catch the fear! Catch the thoughts like...like fish. *Don't look at them! Throw them back into the black! The black.*

The awful feeling subsided a little, and then a little more. His breathing slowed. He was able to look round again.

As the fear ebbed, he was suddenly filled with sexual tension: through the swaying bodies and across the aisle, he saw a pair of rounded knees, broad thighs, flattened by the tram seat. A short, fawn, uniform skirt, like those worn by shopgirls, rode high near the groin.

He shifted sideways surreptitiously. The open knees swung toward him with the motion of the tram. He caught the vee of white panties. He leaned sideways to see more. *God! What am I doing? This is perving!*

But anything was better than the *fear*. Curiously, as his fear lessened, his excitement grew. He slipped his hand into his pocket and touched his penis. The mass of people swung round him. A basket pressed into his back. The plump legs opened a little more. With the clarity of hallucination he saw a light shadow of pubic hair through the thin fabric. *Can't she* feel *me looking? Just a bit more, please!*

The tram stopped. The crowd shuffled forward. The knees straightened, the skirt dropped and the woman got up. With a shock, he saw that she was middle-aged.

He rose quickly, pushed through to the doors and jumped off the tram before they closed.

As he reached the pavement he saw that he had come a little too far; across the road, the huge bulk of the town hall rose white and radiant, like an inner-suburban Ministry of Truth. He averted his eyes and crossed the busy road like a sleepwalker, his mind busy with new discoveries: he could control his mind. He could stop the fear. He could take the ugly frightening thoughts, grab them and push them down into the blackness. What was in the blackness he didn't know. Did all the fears collect and wait? Or did they die?

And if it got too much, if he couldn't capture and dispose of the evil, then he could *swamp* it with something stronger. He thought of the woman on the tram, then of Sophie, with a fierce hard lust.

175

Sex! Yes, that was useful. But so was anger, and—most useful—a steady coldness, a tense callous numbness.

Every time he performed this mental exorcism it got easier. He became more skilful.

He passed the Lebanese delicatessen.

Wonder if Yanni paid them yet—was it only last night?

Then the thought came, half pleasure, half fear:

I killed him. Me. *And I hid him and nobody will know!*

He held the thought for a second and then pushed it away and back.

He turned the corner, walked up to the club, unlocked the door and went through into the kitchen. All without thinking or faltering.

The lights were on. The kitchen was quite normal, rather cleaner than usual. He paused, summoned up that icy numbness and walked to the bench and stood looking at the floor: nothing.

He opened the coolroom. Potato bags lay scattered, away from the wall. He stacked them neatly and returned to the kitchen. On the bench were loaves of sliced bread, cartons of eggs and a few salamis. Pushed to one side lay his cooking tools, still laid out on their cloth.

He looked around again. Nothing. *Nothing.*

On Saturdays he had only to make sandwiches for a couple of hours in the afternoon. For some reason Saturday night was always quiet and Yanni closed most of the club—Carl didn't have to work.

He folded back his sleeves, cleared the bench and laid out rows of sliced bread, chalky white in the fluorescent light. Opening a tub of cheap margarine, he methodically plastered the slices, concentrating on his work, keeping that cool detachment. He looked at his hands, they moved smoothly, without a tremor...then he stopped. He saw that his right hand held an old table knife.

My knife! Where's...? Dave's *got it—it's all right.* (*Catch the thought, push it back!*) He worked on.

He was slicing salami awkwardly with the blunt knife when Yanni walked in.

'Hi, Cookie, you're looking pretty sharp today.'

'Yeah, I had to...'

Yanni turned without listening and shouted:

'Through here! Come on!'

A thin, dark woman sidled in, a little boy following her; although she seemed quite young, her face was lined and her shoulders were stooped. She wore a long, shabby coat and a scarf wrapped round her head. She smiled tentatively.

Carl looked at the little boy. His round cropped head, his expression...he quickly put the knife down and gripped the bench. *He looks like...!*

177

'Listen, Cookie,' said Yanni, 'this is Mustafa's missus and kid. You know Mustafa? Well, he hasn't been home and that and I was telling them we hadn't seen him. Isn't that right?'

Carl couldn't speak. There was a pause. The woman bent to the boy and whispered in his ear. Carl caught the throaty Turkish vowels.

'My mum says you seen my dad, Mustafa Cuyuk?'

Carl looked into the woman's eyes. They shone with unshed tears. A great surge of…pity? fear?…rose in him. With a huge effort he drove it back.

His hands relaxed and he said calmly, 'No, I haven't seen him since…when was it, Yanni?'

'Last week, Cookie. Yeah, that's right. Listen, kid, tell your mum, don't worry, he'll be back…he's probably out gettin' whacked or something.'

The woman bent to the little boy again:

'Mum says…'

'OK. Come on now,' Yanni broke in. 'Cookie's busy.'

He ushered them out. Carl went on slicing sausage mechanically.

He conjured up a wave of anger and contempt. *Bloody wogs, why can't they leave me alone?*

Like an echo he heard Yanni's voice as he came back:

'Bloody Turks! I didn't tell them nothing… he *was* here last night. Trying to get in. You hear? But fuck 'em, they'll get nothing out of me.' Yanni paused

178

and crammed an egg sandwich into his mouth. He looked embarrassed. 'Listen, Cookie, I got some bad news.'

Carl looked up.

'Yeah...ah...it was all right last night, but we're a bit short on...we got a *liquidity problem*, yeah, and anyway we're going to have to close for a while. Know what I mean? So I...'

'Yanni,' Carl cut in, 'where's my pay?' He looked at Yanni coldly.

'Here it is, mate, *and* a bit extra. I'll give you a ring when we open again, OK?'

'You haven't got my phone number,' Carl smiled. He looked steadily into Yanni's shifty eyes. The Greek looked away.

'Well, you ring me, OK? That's enough sangers, you can go if you want to—see you in a couple of weeks.'

He left hurriedly.

Carl laughed a little. It sounded strange in the empty kitchen. He rolled up his tools and, without turning, walked steadily out of the kitchen door, down the passage and home in the hot afternoon.

FOUR

At three o'clock one Sunday morning, about three weeks after Mustafa's sudden end and impromptu interment, Carl was dreaming. The first part of the dream was quite pleasant: he was flying, or was it skating? He couldn't tell. He could see nothing, and all he could feel was the wind against his face as he plunged swiftly forward.

He heard faint music from ahead. It was somehow Oriental but with western melodies, a bit like Borodin but folksier. It was unfamiliar but interesting. He abandoned himself to the movement.

Almost imperceptibly he was slowing down. He felt the first touch of fear.

Coming to a standstill, he hovered in the darkness. Dim yellow circles appeared, spinning with the music, growing brighter and then coalescing into a ring of light, unbearably bright, like a spotlight. He could see tiny motes drifting in the beam.

Into the circle came a bent figure, stooping, its hand held above its head. It was dancing.

The music grew louder and faster. Loose clothes flapping, the figure turned and capered. It raised its round head and grinned: Mustafa.

The music grew frantic. Mustafa, his feet flying, waved and beckoned. Carl tried desperately to wake up. Mustafa beckoned again, but not to Carl. Carl knew who was coming.

On the edge of the bright circle he saw its grey-white rags and one narrow tattered foot.

He woke, crying hoarsely. He lay rigid in his bed, his eyes straining into the dark. The door opened. Against the dim light, he saw the pale thin hair, the white draperies hanging—he screamed.

'What is it, dear? Carl! Are you all right?'

'Oh Mother! Oh *God*!'

She sat on the bed. Blindly he lifted himself and fell into her arms. She patted his head awkwardly.

'Dear, you're shaking.'

'I had this *dream*. Jesus, Mother, I thought you were...'

She held him, his cheek against her pendulous breast.

'What's wrong, dear? Tell me.'

He drew back, ashamed and alarmed.

'No, Mother, I'm all right, it was just a bad dream.'

'What *is* it, dear? Is there something bothering you? You've been so quiet lately.'

'I'm not sleeping too well, that's all.'

'Do you want one of my sleeping pills, dear?'

'I don't know, Mother, they're not too strong, are they?'

'No, dear. I'll just give you one. You'll feel much better.' She got up and left.

He lay back, fighting his mind.

It's not fair—they sneak up on you! They wait till you're asleep.

His mother came back, switching on the light. She held the vial of pills and a glass of water.

'I *can* only give you one, dear. I seem to be nearly out of them…here you are.'

He swallowed the pill eagerly.

'Thanks, Mother. Sorry to wake you.'

'That's all right. I'll wait till you go off again, shall I?'

'No, no. Really. I'll be all right.' Carl was terrified of talking in his sleep. 'You go back to bed…You going to church tomorrow?'

'Yes, dear, of course…' she hesitated. 'Why don't you come…if there's something worrying you…'

'I might just do that.' He felt drowsy. 'Yeah, I *will*.'

'Dear, I *am* pleased.' She bent and kissed him. 'Good night, Carl.'

'Good night Mother. Listen, I…'

'Yes, dear?'

'Ah…nothing.'

*

Mrs Fitzgerald knelt heavily beside her bed. She pushed away the mat and planted her knees painfully on the cold lino, offering up the discomfort, her eyes on the little picture of the virgin propped on her bedside table.

She started a Rosary. As she went mechanically through the Hail Marys, she spoke directly to the picture, her mind wandering a little. She was very tired.

'Dear Mother of God, I'm praying to you for my son. Let him be happy, please. That's all I ask. I know it's my fault—the way he is. We spoilt him when he was a little boy. I couldn't help it—he was such a dear. I remember him so well…in the garden at Sackville Street, playing with his sister. He looked so sweet. But then when he grew up he wouldn't do what I wanted. He was so naughty—and his father passed away and I couldn't control him. Holy Mother, I know he would have been a better man if I had had the money to send him through college. He could have been a doctor or a lawyer or even a chemist. Look at Doctor Lee with his beautiful suits. Now he's a chef. I know he hates it. He looks so tired, poor boy. I know he's rude to me but he can't help it. I'm an old woman. I nag him. *I* can't help it.

183

Now he's got something awful on his mind. I mustn't be worried, Holy Mother, you know that. Please don't let it be anything shameful. I hope it's nothing to do with that girl who rings up. Sophie, is it? I do wish he was still with dear Prue. She was so sensible, and dear little Lilly—you'll look after her, won't you? It's hard when you can't see your grandchild. Let me see her before…Maybe it would be better if it happened soon, then he would have his grandfather's money. But I'm *frightened*. You know what the pain's like and the being sick…Dear Holy Mother, I'm too tired to finish the Rosary but…'

She started the Litany, losing her way in the ancient praises.

'Tower of the Sea—no, that's not right.'

Gasping a little, she lowered her shoulders to the edge of the bed and pulled herself up onto it. Her heart was thumping irregularly, and there was a deep pain starting under her arm.

She lay breathing deeply as her doctor had taught her. She turned painfully and took a pill bottle from the bedside table, knocking over the holy picture. Her heart leapt and twisted, and a pressure built up under her chest. Crossing herself fumblingly, she slipped a tablet under her tongue.

It always seemed a miracle…Soon her heart fell into a smoother rhythm. The pain retreated—waiting.

She straightened the picture.

'Thank you, dear...' She sighed.

Exhausted, she lay on her back. Her nightie rucked up, her thick ruined legs showing. How they throbbed!

That was old age. Lots of small pains leading up to one big one—but it was just as well it was like that, otherwise how would anyone bear the last agony without...what was the word? The sin?...*Despair*.

She hauled herself up in the bed, got under the clothes and composed herself for sleep, crossing her arms on her breast as the nuns had taught her. She remembered Carl's malicious glee when he had seen her like this. He had told her, laughing, that the sisters had wanted you to do this to stop you...she couldn't even think about what he had said...sometimes he was very bad.

She reached over to the table again, for her sleeping pills.

Only three left? She was puzzled. Still, her memory wasn't very good these days...

She took a pill and turned out the light.

As the drowsiness came, she thought, as she often did, of her heart attack. With the pill doing its work she could think about that time without horror.

She had been to her brother John's for dinner and her daughter had worried her all night, snapping and baiting her son-in-law. They hadn't been happy together for some time.

She had smoked too much and yes, she supposed she had had too much wine. She felt ill and they went home early. When she had got home she had been sick. But not just once...terrible bouts of vomiting till she had groaned like an animal. She remembered with shame how she had been sick over her daughter's hands as they held a bowl.

Then the bad pain started...like...like...she knew it was stupid but it felt just like someone was trying to squeeze a tennis ball through a narrow pipe in her chest; at every push, the pain grew worse.

Then the ambulance had arrived. The men called her 'darling' and carried her down the stairs, flopping like an old doll.

Then the oxygen and the needles and she knew she wasn't going to die just yet...And it was funny, but it was only then that she could pray properly. It all seemed like years ago...but it wasn't.

She turned her head and looked at the luminous crucifix on the wall; her son-in-law had given it to her.

'Such bad taste, but he's a good man—I'm sorry, our Lord, but I can't pray to you tonight. I don't feel I *know* you.' Anyway, she thought, her inhibitions weakened by the sleeping pill, you probably worried your mother too!

*

At ten the next morning, Mrs Fitzgerald was putting on her face for Mass. She squinted shortsightedly into the

186

steamy mirror and wiped it with an annoyed gesture. *Really, this bathroom is a disgrace. Still it's better than when I came.*

She had put up a new shower curtain and cleaned the crust of ages from the bath, but it was still squalid.

She smoothed a thick layer of liquid make-up over her nose and cheeks and down over her chins. *Dear, I am getting stout again. But I do look better.*

After the heart attack her flesh had melted away alarmingly, leaving the skin hanging in ugly folds.

She put on her lipstick. *What a pretty mouth I had…It was so soft.*

Now her lips seemed to have shrunk and thinned; this puzzled her since she still had all her own teeth. *I must get that boy to the dentist.*

Powdering her face vigorously, she looked at her reflection. *Nothing the matter with that!*

She fluffed up her thin hair, sprayed it and put on her dressing gown.

Going through the kitchen, on her way to dress, she lit a cigarette. *Where's that boy?*

'Time to get up dear…we'll be late.'

There was silence from Carl's room; she knocked briskly and went into her bedroom.

Opening her underwear drawer, she considered and then took out her best long-line corset. Puffing a little, she eased it on…how it did hurt! Grunting as she pulled it up, her eyes caught the mild, compassionate gaze from the bedside table.

I can't very well offer this up, now can I? It's very uncomfortable—still, I don't want the boy to be ashamed of his old mother.

She rearranged herself in the lycra and pulled on her support stockings. She caught sight of her back view in the wardrobe mirror.

Oh dear, I do look a figure of fun. Still, with a nice frock…it's not every day your son takes you to church. After all these years!

She put on a grey silk dress, her pearls, and a pair of very high heels. Tottering a little, she went out to wake Carl.

She knocked on his door again.

'Yeah, yeah, *all right* Mother, I'm up, I won't be long.'

She sat down in the living room and looked around with some satisfaction; the curtains were clean and the furniture polished. There was a vase of fresh flowers on a stereo speaker. A new rug covered the grimy sea-grass.

That boy really needs me. She thought of the previous night. *He was rather sweet, just like when he was a little boy. What nightmares he had then—how he used to cry! He still needs a cuddle, even at his age…*

Simple happiness filled her.

And now he's coming to church. If only he'd hurry—I'll get him going!

She smiled to herself and slipped a cassette into the stereo: Mahler's Fifth.

As the trumpets swelled, Carl flung open his bedroom door.

'Oh Mother! For Christ's sake! You know I can't bear that crap.'

He was wearing his blue shirt and narrow dark tie, and his grey trousers.

'Well, it did hurry you up, didn't it dear? You *do* look nice, but you haven't had a shave. Off you go—quickly now!'

Carl peered at her.

'You look very chirpy this morning, Mother.'

'Yes, dear, I'm pleased you're coming to Mass. But I *don't* want to be late, so do hurry.'

Carl went out.

Still, it's only just round the corner.

She lit a Rothman's Plain and sat waving her plump hands to the music.

Carl came back, his pale face marked with the weals of a hasty shave. He flicked the off button on the stereo.

'All right, Mother, got everything? Let's go.'

'Just my bag, dear, and my pills...be a good boy and get them for me. On my bedside table.'

Carl started into her bedroom. The phone rang by his ear. He flinched and stared at it...

'Aren't you going to answer it?'

'Yes, yes, Mother.'

He picked up the receiver. It was Sophie.

'Hello, Carl?'

'Yeah.'

'Listen, Carl, I got to see you, I got to tell you something...'

'Look, I can't for a while, I told you, my mother...'

'No, this is important.'

A pang of fear shot through him—she *couldn't* know anything.

'What is it? Tell me now, for Christ's sake.'

'Carl, I missed my period...and I'm never late... Look, I've got to see you. I'm at Auntie Martha's. She's out...can you come over? I told you about Dad and that. If I have to tell him...You said you...Carl, I *got* to leave home!'

Carl looked at his mother; she was sitting placidly, not listening in a marked manner. The first real hatred rose in him. *You fucking old*...He calmed himself.

'OK, Sophie, look...I'll take care of it! I can't talk now, I have to take Mother to church. Ring me later, OK? Everything'll be all right...trust me.'

'Yeah, OK Carl, but you'll fix it up, won't you? I got no money since the club closed...and I can't get another job.' She was crying.

He felt protective, lustful, fearful and very angry all at once. His voice shook slightly.

190

'Look, *don't worry*, I'll take care of everything…ring me later.'

He put the phone down and stood staring at his mother.

This's all I need. No money. No job. Sophie needs an…And…and that other thing…And this bloody old bitch is still hanging round! Christ! I'd like to…!

He raised that icy numbness…

'What's wrong, dear? Are you all right? You are coming, aren't you? Who was that?'

'It was only Sophie, Mother,' he said calmly, 'you know, that girl from work. She's in a bit of trouble, she…'

'What *kind* of trouble? It's nothing to do with you, is it? I *knew* there was something…'

'No, no, Mother, it's to do with the club, that's all. She just wants my advice. No, everything's fine… we better get going.' *It'll be a good place to think, and I must think.*

He went into his mother's bedroom and picked up her bag and started putting pill bottles into it. A label caught his eye: 'Digoxin—Warning—Do not exceed the prescribed dose'. A vague memory stirred.

Dig…Digit…something—Digitalis!

A thought, an idea leapt like a silver salmon. He caught it. It squirmed in his mind, swam free and vanished. He dropped the vial into the bag and closed it, jumping a little at the snap of the catch.

He went slowly back into the living room.

Better get a book. He remembered the boredom of Mass at school…boredom broken by flashes of beauty, that was how he remembered it.

'All ready, Mother?' He gave her the bag. 'Won't be a tick…I just have to get something.'

He went to the bookcase in his room and rummaged through the tattered paperbacks…*A Dictionary of Drugs.*

It won't hurt just to find out. He stuck it in his pocket.

*

He ushered his mother out of the door and followed her down the path. A hot gritty north wind was blowing. Her skirt flew above her knees; she staggered a little and turned to him. Her face was damp already, the powder clumping on her cheeks.

'Oh dear, it *is* warm. Give me your arm, Carl. Such a mercy it's so close.'

He looked at her with contempt. *How absurd she looks—those stupid shoes! Christ!*

'All right Mother…off we go.'

He took her arm and they stepped out.

He flinched with revulsion at the touch of her arm; the flesh was loose and flabby. He quickened his pace.

'Please, Carl, not so fast.' She was wheezing.

'Well, we'll be late, Mother. I don't want everybody looking at us.'

'I *am* glad you're coming, though, dear.'

'Yeah, OK, Mother.'

At least I can think there—I must think—I must look at things.

After about ten minutes they turned into Blyth Street. The church was over the road. As they waited to cross she turned to him, pressing his arm.

'What I meant to say, Carl, was—I wish you wouldn't have anything to do with those girls.'

'What girls, Mother, for God's sake?'

'Ones like the one who rang up...You won't, dear, will you? Now I want you to write to dear Prue after church...you will, won't you? You need someone to look after you and I won't be...Now I'm relying on you, Carl, I do want you to settle down, otherwise I'll have to speak to your Uncle John. You know what I mean by that, don't you?'

He looked at her.

'Now, dear, don't look like that. I only want to see my children settled.'

'OK, OK, come on!'

They crossed the road and approached the church. It was a rather handsome building with a neo-Renaissance tower.

Mrs Fitzgerald paused and took a square of black lace from her bag, draped it over her head and tucked the ends into her dress. The effect was grotesque in the extreme, rather like Toad as the washerwoman.

'God, Mother, what's that?'

'It's a *mantilla*,' she said, a little defensively. 'I know you don't have to wear a hat any more, but...what's wrong with it?'

'I don't know...you look like one of those Turkish ladies...' He thought of Mustafa's wife and shook himself. 'Never mind, Mother. Let's get inside. It's started. I can hear singing.'

They went inside, Carl following his mother, automatically dipping his fingers into holy water and crossing himself.

Jesus! How long has it been? At school, was it? He looked around bewildered; the church was extremely simple, bare even. *Where's the statues?*

The alter was a block of stained pine with what looked like a lurex flecked polyester curtain draped across it. Two lecterns stood at either side and at the back a flimsy stand with a plain metal box on it—a crude pottery cup beside. To the right, on the wall, was a large board with numbers slotted into it.

A young man in a tracksuit played an electric organ. The thinly scattered congregation was singing raggedly—an English hymn! It sounded like...was it 'Rock of Ages' or 'All Creatures Great and Small'?

'Mother!' he whispered urgently, 'for God's sake, this is the wrong church! It's *Baptist* or something.'

'Don't be silly, Carl.' She genuflected and sat down. Clumsily he followed her. 'This is how it is now. Really dear, how long since…shush now. It's starting.'

A grey-haired woman in a shapeless floral dress walked to the lectern, followed by a fat youngish man with a shock of black curls. He was wearing a short robe? vestment? of the same material as the altar cloth. The lurex sparkled in the pale light. He sat down behind and to one side of the altar. Carl was surprised to see that he was wearing shorts and sandals under his robe. He had very hairy legs.

The grey-haired woman started to read from a plastic folder. Carl could make out only a word or two. He glanced at his mother. She was slumped with her head in her hands, praying, he supposed.

He looked about again. There were perhaps fifty or sixty people in the big church. Most were elderly. There were a few Italian families at the back with young children. He was surprised again at how bare it all was. The walls were unadorned except for a line of small ugly blue plaques ranged along both sides—they looked like china ducks. He squinted at them.

They look like…yes, Stations of the Cross! It is a Catholic Church! And those windows—they must be the original stained glass.

A soft pale lemon and rose light shone through them. The effect was soothing. Carl relaxed a little. He was tired.

What a dream. He shuddered, remembering the previous night. *As long as I don't talk in my sleep. She's not as deaf as I thought...Jesus—I nearly told her! She'll have to go back to South Yarra...or something.*

The grey-haired woman finished speaking and sat down. The tracksuited boy stood behind the other lectern and began to read in a nasal monotone. Carl fidgeted restlessly. Ideas, fearful, ugly, but inviting, twisted through his mind.

He reached into his back pocket and eased out the book, glancing again at his mother. She was still praying. *Better hide the cover.*

He picked up a yellow leaflet from the seat beside him and folded it round the paperback. Bending forward in an attitude of devotion, he turned to the index.

'Digoxin'—page seventy—OK. Digitalis. Classification—from foxgloves—well, well. 'Therapeutic use of Digitalis is in the treatment of congestive heart failure.' There followed a short biochemical treatise of which Carl could understand very little. He turned the page. 'Side effects. In large doses, on or after the cumulative effects of long term treatment, Digitalis and all the other cardiac glycosides can produce fatal intoxication. The most frequent cause of death is increase in heart arrhythmias, leading to atrial and ventricular fibrillation. Death is due, in fact, to arrhythmic heart failure.'

He turned another page. There was a sectional drawing of a heart. He looked at his mother. *No! I can't.* His hand shaking, he put the book away.

No! Don't let me...

The shiny little thoughts kept showing their heads. With a practised effort he pushed them down and sat back, trying to keep his mind blank. The thoughts kept coming and coming...There was awful pain and guilt in them but also, and horrifyingly, a slow lascivious pleasure.

He stared rigidly ahead, his teeth clenched. He felt someone sit down next to him. He couldn't look or move. Sweat trickled down his back like blood.

His mother nudged him. He gasped in shock:

'Ah!'

'Shush, dear. Stand up, it's the Gospel.'

The fat priest was speaking in a rich Irish tenor.

'This is the word of the Lord!'

Carl stood, formless images crowding his mind, the amplified voice rolling round him:

'I shall separate the sheep from the goats...'

At last the voice stopped. There was a pause. His mother pulled him down. He sat numbly.

Suddenly the sun shone overwhelmingly through the nearest stained glass window. Carl was bathed in a wonderful golden light. Motes sparkled in the beams.

Just like my dream! He stared into the radiance, transfixed.

And into the nimbus: 'Now, my dear brothers and sisters, I'd like to say a few words to you about *forgiveness*!' The priest's voice carolled out joyfully. 'Yes, *forgiveness*. For today is the Feast of Christ the King— Christ the Judge. But not a judge like our earthly judges. No, brothers and sisters, not the corrupt, severe and worldly judges we see about us! But a heavenly judge! Friendly, merciful and forgiving. Yes, *all forgiving*.' The voice dropped confidentially. 'I'd like to tell you a little story now. A recent experience of mine. The other day, in fact, a man came to me in an agony of spirit, yes, literally *agony*…For years he had been an *abortionist*. Yes. An *abortionist*, a murderer of infants. In those years he had killed hundreds, nay, thousands of innocent little babies…In a way, brothers and sisters, he was worse than a *Nazi* in one of those terrible death camps. Suddenly he realised what he was doing; the heinous sin of it. And he was in an *agony* of grief and remorse…he thought that he could *never* be forgiven.

'Now, I can't tell you this man's name, but the first part of it rhymes with Cain—yes, Cain, the first murderer…Now this man came to me in fear and despair. He had lost *all* hope of reconciliation with God and the Church. I tell you, brothers and sisters, this man was *desperate*.

'But I was able to tell him, assure him, *counsel him*, that our Heavenly Father will forgive anything! Even a heinous sin like his…Now isn't that a wonderful thing! A sin like that washed away in the holy blood!'

Carl felt his mind spinning slowly away. The light surrounded him like a fiery cloud…the voice boomed on, but he heard no more…the light grew blinding. He put his hands to his face. He could see nothing.

*

The sun shifted and the light dimmed. He took his hands away from his face, blinking cautiously. It was all right. He saw.

The priest was saying: 'Now let us pray for the dead. May we meet them in the flesh, face to face.'

Yes—I could now. He felt calm and resolute. *What's happened to me?* It was like in the grave-yard…*Something…went…But it feels* good *now. Do I believe in Christ and all that? I never used to—but now? I can feel someone. He knows! He doesn't care— He's forgiven me—even before I…*

The boy in the tracksuit came round with a plate, people dropping money into it. Carl took out all the notes in his pocket and leant across the back of a short dark man kneeling next to him. He threw the notes into the plate…

There were more prayers. Carl vaguely recognized the Gloria in English. The priest's voice rang out again.

'Peace be with you!'

199

The congregation turned to one another and shook hands…Carl took his mother's hand and smiled at her. She frowned at him worriedly.

'You all right, dear?'

'Yes, Mother.'

He turned to the man next to him. The man grinned, holding out his hand. It was Mustafa…

Carl looked at him, into his dark eyes; they shone with happiness.

'Peace be with you, and with your spirit!' said Mustafa…There was an echo: *'I forgive you.'*

Carl took the man's hand. No, of course it wasn't Mustafa. He wasn't even very much like him, but it meant something. *All this did.*

He looked toward the altar. People were lining up taking Communion.

How beautiful everything was! The church had changed its geometry in a queer way. It seemed longer…loftier…How could he have thought this place drab? How clear the colours were!

His mother got up.

'Excuse me, dear.'

She got out of the pew with difficulty and waddled up the aisle. He watched her, smiling.

How old *she has gotten lately—Ah! It would be a…mercy. After all, she's very sick.* He was washed by a languorous pity. *She won't mind—Mustafa doesn't mind…*

The communicants returned. His mother sat down again puffing, her hand to her chest.

'Dear, I think we can go now. I feel a little frail.'

'Yes, of course, Mother.'

They pushed past Carl's neighbour.

Strange—he really isn't anything like…No, it was a vision—it really meant something! He was exalted.

He reached the top of the low stone steps outside the church door. His mother waited.

'Come on, dear. I really must go home.'

'Yes, Mother…wait a bit.'

He looked around.

How *wonderful* it all was. Why, Brunswick was beautiful! The sun glanced and bounced off the cars whizzing past. How *shiny* they were…he had never realized how many different clear, lovely colours cars were. And the trees! He could see every leaf so distinctly…the shades of green were…*delicious.*

The sky wasn't just blue but…like in an old painting from the Middle Ages. What was the word? *Cerulean…* yes. And the sun…He looked into it without pain and away slowly. His eyes filled with tears of joy.

Everything seemed as if it were *meant.* No longer did he feel as if he were part of some tawdry accident…he felt part of something ordered, deliberate.

He walked down gracefully and took his mother's arm.

'Can we get a taxi, dear? I know it's not far but I don't think I can...'

'Of course, Mother.'

He raised his hand. A taxi stopped immediately. He nodded to himself—yes.

They got in and his mother gave the address.

'Carl,' she said, 'I hope you weren't offended by what I said before.'

'No, Mother, you can't offend me.'

'That's good, dear. You know I want what's best for you.'

'Do you, Mother? That's nice.'

He looked at her benevolently. *How small she is— silly little woman.*

She was talking. He watched her thin, sunken mouth moving mechanically in her flabby cheeks. Distantly he heard her say:

'You do seem better after church, Carl. More relaxed...I knew you would.'

'Oh yes,' said Carl, 'I feel much better.'

'Oh dear!' she said, gasping a little. 'I wish I could say the same...I better take a pill.'

She fumbled with the catch on her bag.

'No, Mother,' he said, smiling, holding her hand. 'You wait. I'll put you into bed and bring you a cup of tea and you'll feel better. Why don't you give me your bag...I'll carry it.'

'That's a good boy.'

He could hear her wheezing.

As the taxi turned into Carl's street, he looked out the window and saw Dave and June. She was pushing a pram...Dave was limping heavily.

He looked at them incuriously, his face calm. Actually, he wasn't quite sure who they were.

The taxi pulled up.

Will it be now? he thought luxuriously. *Or will I just* wish *it to happen.*

He helped his mother out and up the front path...

*

As Dave and June turned into Carl's street, they were arguing.

'Why the hell did we have to come so far, Dave? You *know* you shouldn't be walking on that leg!' Dave's leg had been in a plastic brace since the day he had fallen in the cemetery. 'And why do we have to come this way, for Christ's sake? This is Carl's street, isn't it? I don't want to see the little creep. You still haven't explained what...'

'Just shut up, June,' Dave said, limping along, new lines of pain in his face. 'I just wanted...Jesus! There he is!'

The taxi drove past, Carl looking out blank-faced.

'Here! Stop, hon, June! Stop, wait!'

Dave stood still, watching the car stop and Carl help his mother out.

Dave strained to see the fifty yards between him and Carl.

'Shit!' he muttered.

'Dave, what's wrong?'

'Shut up!'

He bent urgently forward, his bad leg braced.

The way Carl had his arm across her shoulders! There was something...He was like a...like a *praying mantis! Jesus! No...*

Dave saw Carl look up into the sun, smiling. He and his mother went into the house. The door closed.

Dave shook his head violently. He beat his fist against his knee. *I'll* have *to tell them...*

'No!'

'Look, Dave,' she said, with love and exasperation, 'what's *wrong?*'

Dave gazed at her, his face suffering.

'Come home, June...I got to tell you something.'

Text Classics

The Commandant
Jessica Anderson
Introduced by Carmen Callil

Homesickness
Murray Bail
Introduced by Peter Conrad

Sydney Bridge Upside Down
David Ballantyne
Introduced by Kate De Goldi

Bush Studies
Barbara Baynton
Introduced by Helen Garner

A Difficult Young Man
Martin Boyd
Introduced by Sonya Hartnett

The Cardboard Crown
Martin Boyd
Introduced by Brenda Niall

The Australian Ugliness
Robin Boyd
Introduced by Christos Tsiolkas

All the Green Year
Don Charlwood
Introduced by Michael McGirr

The Even More Complete
Book of Australian Verse
John Clarke
Introduced by John Clarke

Diary of a Bad Year
J. M. Coetzee
Introduced by Peter Goldsworthy

Wake in Fright
Kenneth Cook
Introduced by Peter Temple

The Dying Trade
Peter Corris
Introduced by Charles Waterstreet

They're a Weird Mob
Nino Culotta
Introduced by Jacinta Tynan

The Songs of a Sentimental Bloke
C. J. Dennis
Introduced by Jack Thompson

Careful, He Might Hear You
Sumner Locke Elliott
Introduced by Robyn Nevin

Terra Australis
Matthew Flinders
Introduced by Tim Flannery

My Brilliant Career
Miles Franklin
Introduced by Jennifer Byrne

The Fringe Dwellers
Nene Gare
Introduced by Melissa Lucashenko

Cosmo Cosmolino
Helen Garner
Introduced by Ramona Koval

Dark Places
Kate Grenville
Introduced by Louise Adler

The Long Prospect
Elizabeth Harrower
Introduced by Fiona McGregor

The Watch Tower
Elizabeth Harrower
Introduced by Joan London